PRAISE FOR *SAMAN*

"...an impressive work, written in a fresh, lively prose shifting
among different times and locations."
International Herald Tribune

"...simply impossible to put down...[Utami] is one of the
most promising young writers to emerge in
Indonesia over the last decade."
Inside Indonesia

"...compelling storytelling, told through
different perspectives, using a range of literary
genres and contemporary writings."
Vrij Nederland

"*Saman* is constructed like a post-modern collage...
the complex story is told multi-voiced."
Onze Wereld

AYU UTAMI

a novel

TRANSLATED BY PAMELA ALLEN

EQUINOX
PUBLISHING
JAKARTA   SINGAPORE

PT Equinox Publishing Indonesia
Menara Gracia 6/F
Jl. HR Rasuna Said Kav. C-17
Jakarta 12940
Indonesia

www.EquinoxPublishing.com

Saman
by Ayu Utami
translated by Pamela Allen

This translation was supported by the Australian Society of Authors

ISBN 979-3780-11-8
©2005 Ayu Utami

First Equinox Edition 2005

Originally published in the Indonesian language by
Kepustakaan Populer Gramedia in 1998
with ISBN 979-9023-17-3 under the title *Saman*

Printed in the United States.

1 3 5 7 9 10 8 6 4 2

a note on the translation

When I began reading *Saman* soon after its publication in 1998, I couldn't put it down. The novel took hold of me in many ways and for many reasons. It wasn't only the narratorial style that takes the reader on a marvellous meandering journey through time and space. It wasn't only the wonderfully crafted characters that come alive on every page. It wasn't only the bold engagement with Indonesian socio-political realities. It was all of the above plus perhaps most of all the language – language that is at once lyrical and descriptive, language that achieves just the right mix of metaphor, metonymy and realism, language that draws you in yet keeps you alert.

When I took on the task of translating the novel into English, the most difficult challenge was to keep that enticing linguistic mélange. I had to find the right tone, the right style and of course the right words to endow Laila with her dreamy naive romanticism, Yasmin with her brusque (yet somehow brittle) efficiency, Shakuntala with her sometimes confronting boldness, Saman with his sensitive humanity and wavering faith. More than that, I had to achieve what Ayu Utami does so well in Indonesian – a cinematographic effect, whereby the narrator describes what is, without attempting to explain or interpret, whereby the reader is presented with a visual panorama rather than a plot-driven narrative, whereby the subject is effectively removed from the text.

Thus began a long, arduous, but ultimately thoroughly rewarding process, which entailed much pondering, revising and tinkering. Most importantly, it also involved much collaboration with Ayu. That process began with the very first sentence of the novel. Initially I joined the first two sentences together, feeling that it created a better "flow" in English. However, as Ayu pointed out, "flow" is an irrelevant concept in this particular paragraph. The first sentence, like many others in the novel, needs to be short, sharp, to the point.

Inevitably I sometimes fell into the trap of explanation – and I thank Ayu for pulling me out of it. As Willis Barnstone points out, explanation should be left to the critic, not the translator. For the translator, explanation is "heresy".[1]

Another pitfall was my tendency to political correctness. I wanted, for example, to rescue Laila from her historical ignorance, by making her say, ironically "I hadn't realised Hitler was a Communist", whereas she in truth has no idea whether Hitler was a Communist or not. Similarly, the temptation was to tone down Anson's anti-Chinese diatribe rather than let his words bear witness to a widespread and deeply-held resentment of the Chinese in Indonesia.

And then there were the metaphors. Here the translator is faced with a number of options. If she is lucky there is an equivalent metaphor, one with the same meaning and from the same semantic field – such as Sihar being "like a wild horse that doesn't care for the orderly life of the farm." More often though, there is the need to find a different metaphor with the same meaning – *tanak seperti nasi* thus becomes "bread fresh from the oven", for example. The least desirable option for the translator is the paraphrase, whereby the meaning of the metaphor is conveyed in different words. This is tantamount to the "heresy" of explanation and the metaphor gets lost in the translation. When translating *Saman* I spent a considerable amount of time and energy working with Ayu on metaphors, on trying to convey both the meaning and the lyrical quality of the original Indonesian tropes. The publication of *Saman* generated considerable debate and discussion, not to say controversy, surrounding its explicit sexual context. However, as the translator I was still faced with the problem of what to do about euphemism. If metaphors do not comfortably cross cultural barriers, then euphemisms often appear completely culture-bound. In this area, too, the translator needs to work closely with the author to ascertain the reasons for the use of euphemism in a particular context. The conversations between Laila and Sihar, for example, are often imbued with a rich euphemistic sub-text that requires a carefully nuanced translation.

Leza Lowitz has likened the art of translation to midwifery.[2] While the analogy may seem a little corporeal (and would the metaphor work in Indonesian?), it is nonetheless apt. In the process of ensuring the safe delivery of this "new life" I was helped by many people. My thanks of course go to Ayu Utami, for entrusting her progeny to me, and for her painstaking assistance in the process of translation. I am also grateful to those colleagues and students who made constructive comments about the translation in its draft form. Finally my thanks to Mark Hanusz for taking it on as a publishing venture.

Pam Allen
Hobart, August 2005

1   Willis Barnstone, "The Poem behind the Poem: Literary Translation as American Poetry", in *Silenced Voices: New Writing from Indonesia*, eds Frank Stewart & John McGlynn, *Manoa*, University of Hawaii Press, 2000, p. 79

2   "Midwifing the Underpoem" in *Silenced Voices: New Writing from Indonesia*, eds Frank Stewart & John McGlynn, *Manoa*, University of Hawaii Press, 2000, p. 105

acknowledgements

I would like to thank Pam Allen who started the translation from her genuine interest in the book and who has gone through the process full of dedication. Also to Eddin Khoo, whose previous collaboration with me in an effort to translate the "ogre story" greatly influenced the final draft. To Janet Steele, for her editing of the final translation. To my publisher Mark Hanusz and adviser Orlow Seunke, for their wonderful cooperation. To Andang Binawan, Erik Prasetya and Kirk Coningham, for their different kinds of help.

Thanks again those who assisted and supported me when I wrote the original work in Indonesian: Budi Hadi Totok Priyono, Badung Baroto, Emilia Susiati, Goenawan Mohamad, Heru Hendratmoko, Nasiruddin, Nicky Satriyo, Prasetyohadi, Sijo Sudarsono, Sitok Srengenge and Tony Prabowo.

CENTRAL PARK, 28 MAY 1996

Here in this park I'm a bird that's flown thousands of miles from a country that knows no seasons, a bird that's migrated in search of spring; spring, where you can smell the grass and the trees; trees, whose name or ages we can never know.

The aroma of wood, the coldness of stone, the smell of moss and mushrooms – do these things have a name, do they have an age? Man gives them names, as parents give their children names, although the trees are older than man. *Rafflesia arnoldi* blooms not in Central Park but in the tropical forest of the Malay highlands and we know its father is an Englishman because he has given the flower its name. People talk about things that grow, both cultivated and native, as if they know them more than the trees know about coldness and sun, or about the warmth of the earth. But animals don't recognize the woods by their names, just as a mother animal or mating pair have no names for their chicks or cubs. They know without language.

In this park the animals are simply contented, as I myself am, a tourist in New York. Does beauty have need of a name?

Ten AM.

The day is young but the shadows are shrinking, for as spring draws on the days are getting longer. Small birds seek the sun through the gaps in the leaves, allowing its rays to heat their passion until lust blossoms, warm as bread fresh from the oven. Some of these birds, whose voices are already raised in song, will find a mate this season. Like that petite white-breasted pair over there, the male with his dark brown cape, the female with her pale brown one. We don't know their names; we only know that they are contented. Does beauty have need of a name?

A tramp stretched out on the bench squirms in his grimy blanket. We don't know who he is. What is the color of his skin. But we know that he is enjoying his sleep. I'm happy, that will be my answer if he wakes up and asks me any questions. Even if he talks in his dream. I'm going to have an encounter with my lover, just like the white-breasted bird on the branch of that tree. I'm going to be embraced, I'm going to be kissed, we'll walk, we'll drink tea in the Russian Tea Room a few blocks away to the south west. A bit expensive, but what the hell. It will be just this once.

Because I'm waiting here for Sihar. Here, unbeknownst to anyone apart from the tramp. Away from any parents, away from any wife. Away from those moral judges or the police. Here, people, particularly tourists, can do as the birds do: mate when they feel the desire. No regrets afterwards. No sin.

And when he gets here I'll show him the sketches I did when I was longing for him so much. And the poems beneath them. *I yearn for the hungry mouth / of a man whose youth is gone / left behind in the sand where he has sought his fortune.* I wrote that on a watercolor. A painting of an oil refinery in the ocean wave, probably. Paintings and poems require neither definition nor explanation. They are repositories for feelings. And for beauty, perhaps.

And when he gets here and sees the sketches, he will know how much I have missed the ardor of his embrace, the warmth of his tongue with the flavor of Skoal tobacco. He enjoys smoking but he doesn't indulge in it out of respect for those who detest cigarette smoke. These days he just chews black tobacco seeds, sucking but not smoking. He is considerate and this morning it is precisely four hundred and twenty-four days since our last kiss – our last rendezvous. 424 days. April 22 last year. It's a date imprinted on my memory, and I'm forever counting the days. Because the legacies of that day were a taste of bitterness, the sting of bile in the back of the throat, and a longing for another chance. Which could be impossible. (I hope that today it will be a possibility.)

We were in a hotel room. I was shivering with embarrassment and excitement. I'd never been alone in a room with a man before. He was quiet, didn't say whether he'd ever escorted a woman like this before. He was an oil rig worker; he spent months on end out in the jungle or the ocean, where the nearest settlements were tiny hovels with prostitutes in gloomy mold-ridden rooms, or villages where lusty young girls were eager to marry the oil workers. I sensed that he was a little nervous in this room with me, but it was nothing compared to my mortification – I hid in the bathroom when the waiter brought our room service order. Because I was a sinner.

Then we lay on the bed, without taking off the bedspread; after all we weren't there for an afternoon nap. He told me I had big breasts. I said nothing. He asked me if I was ready. I said, "Please don't, I'm a virgin. Could we do it another way?" He said I had beautiful lips. "Kiss me, kiss me here," I responded to him, but there was no need for words. But I had sinned. Even though I was still a virgin.

On the way home he said it would be best if we didn't see each other again. (I wasn't expecting this.) "I'm married."

I replied that I didn't have a boyfriend, but I did have parents. "You're not alone. I'm a sinner too."

He said that was not the point. "Once you're married it's hard to forego sex."

I understood. Even though I was still a virgin.

The next day he was gone. Maybe to the ocean, or to the jungle, to places where people with lots of capital mine dollars from the oil that nature preserves in her anticlinal contour. Maybe he'd gone back to the rig that I had been to, the place where we first met, where the sea made us feel we would drown and the stars made us feel we would lose our way. Just as I lost my way trying to track him down. I tried for months, maybe five months. Until one day out of the blue he phoned me at work.

"Why don't you ever phone me any more?" he asked. "I've tried but I lost track of you," I replied. "I'm still here," he said. And my heart pounded at the thought of him being right here, in Jakarta.

"Can we meet?" I ventured. "For lunch?"

"And after lunch?"

"After lunch, well…by then it could be late afternoon."

"How about dinner?"

"Is your wife away?"

"How did you know? You've been phoning my home haven't you?"

"Sihar, you've never asked me to dinner before…"

He fell silent. I too fell silent.

Then he asked whether we could have breakfast together the next morning if we dined together in the evening. I reminded him that I still lived with my parents. They would ask questions if I didn't come home. "Even though you're an adult and travel frequently?" he said. "Yes," I said, nodding. I could hear him sighing at the other end of the phone. "And on top of all that you're still a virgin." We didn't see each other that night. And the same scenario was repeated over and over again, more than sixteen times. Until one day he told me not to phone him again. "It's for the best," he said. I asked why. "I'm married," he said. I asked why.

"Often when my wife answers the phone the caller hangs up straight away."

"Well it's not me," I lied. (I didn't do it that often.) "Maybe it was someone else?"

"She says it's some sort of premonition."

"See, now you're the one who feels guilty. Even though we've never actually done anything."

And so we still didn't get to see each other. I badly wanted to phone him. How was he feeling? What did his face look like? For two or three months I continued to hope it would be him every time the phone rang, at work or at home. After three months it dawned on me that he was actually showing self-restraint. Who knows why. Maybe he was protecting his wife. Maybe he was protecting himself. He used to say that meeting me would be painful for him, because he would be withholding something he needed to release. Call it lust. "Because once you're married it's hard to forego sex." Maybe I too should be protecting his wife, or him. After all, I wasn't married, so I didn't need to forego it. But I missed him so much. Which one of us should be the one taking feelings into account? In the end it was me who had to take on that responsibility. Because I wasn't married. Because I was the last one on the scene. Three years ago.

SOUTH CHINA SEA, FEBRUARY 1993

From above and from a distance an oil rig looks like a silver box in a sea of lapis lazuli. The helicopter descended and the sea that had seemed calm at first became a seething sheet of water, serene but powerful, as if it were hiding a great force in its depths. The woman signaled to the pilot to circle around so she could get a good camera angle on the towers below. She slid open the window a little and her zoom lens emerged into the low-pressure atmosphere. The wind ruffled her hair, which she wore in a bob with chestnut highlights in deference to the insistent pleas of her hairdresser. The wind whistled, the engines' roar was deafening. Conversation was impossible for the three people inside the chopper. The woman gave the thumbs up after she had taken a few shots, a process that had frozen her fingers. The machine hovered above the water for a moment before landing, creating whirlpools that refracted the light from the sky into tiny fragments like points of pigment in a Seurat painting.

It was searingly hot. The wind was gusting, from the sea and from the helicopter blades. A man emerged from the rim of the bridgehead. He appeared to have climbed up a ladder that seemed to spring straight out of the ocean. No structures from below the helipad were visible behind him. He was clearly not an oil rig worker. He was clean shaven. And he wasn't wearing overalls. He was dressed in cotton shorts and a casual shirt, rather loose. He introduced himself. Rosano, Cano for short. He was a representative of Texcoil, an oil company with exploration rights in the waters around Anambas peninsula. So it was fair to say that he was the landlord of this particular building. He shook hands firmly with the new arrivals and smiled briefly but he made no eye contact. His glance seemed to stop somewhere in mid-air between them. Then his attention was diverted by a man coming towards them from the other side of the bridgehead, bringing safety helmets. He asked them to put them on. It's perfectly safe here, he said, but a seagull could shit on your head, or a sudden movement might make you hit your head on a pole, or make a pole strike you on your head. There's no danger, we just have to take precautions. As the posters say, *Safety first.*

The woman's name was Laila and the man was Tony. They ran a small production company – or partnership more accurately – that had a contract to undertake two connected projects. First to do a profile of Texcoil Indonesia, a joint venture with a mining company based in Canada. They had also been assigned by Petroleum Extension Services to write a book on oil exploration in the Asia-Pacific region. But their host seemed distracted as he hastily explained the drilling process to them. Something was not quite in order. They talked as they walked briskly around the iron and steel construction that stuck out of the ocean, propped up by four jacks. Overalled workers nodded politely to the thirty-something Cano. But there were audible wolf-whistles once they'd passed by. Laila started to feel like an outsider as the only woman in this peculiar place. Peculiar because there was only one woman. *Me.*

On the northern side of the rig a supply boat rocked wildly in the powerful north-eastern current. The thunder of the waves repeatedly drowned out the shouted conversation between those on the boat and those on the platform. Their skin was dark, like that of wharf labourers. They had just finished loading some pallets of equipment onto a gondola dangling from a crane that extended from the platform to the deck of the boat. Seagulls screeched as if they were trying to land on the tip of the poles. Two of the boat's crew attempted to leap into the gondola, which was being held steady by several other men. One jumped, the other hesitated. He was almost washed into the water by a wave. His mate grabbed him by the shoulder when he was safely in the gondola. The giant claw rotated 180 degrees as it transferred its cargo of equipment and men to the platform, which was abuzz with machinery.

"They're from Seismoclypse, the oil service we contract for logging," said Cano as they approached some men putting together a piece of sensoring equipment they had just unloaded from the crane. He referred to them as "service people"; they called him "the company man". The company man, who can dress as he pleases and commands respect, because he is part of the company that's providing all the money. Laila and Tony followed him to where the men were working.

As we approach they all look at me, unable to disguise their interest. Because I am the only woman.

But one of them, the one who had grabbed his mate by the shoulder, seemed utterly indifferent. He gave Laila the most fleeting of glances, glasses flashing, then turned his back and bent down toward the machine, inspecting it. The top of his overall was rolled down to his waist, and she saw that his neck was burnt much darker than his arms. And the arms were muscled from the rigors of hard labor.

I can smell his sweat.

"How are things, Sihar? The job seems to be going pretty slowly," said Rosano, as if he didn't care that he had guests with him.

The man muttered something unintelligible, but finally replied, "I'll have to monitor this instrument for a while longer. It looks as if we won't be able to start the job just yet, sir. The mud logger's analysis indicates rising gas pressure down there. We'll have to wait a bit...*sir*." His deliberately stressed the word "sir", not to show respect, but rather to mock the arrogant Rosano, who enjoyed being addressed in this way. Both men were around the same age, about thirty-five. Rosano may even have been a little younger.

The company man shook his head and clicked his tongue; this was not the answer he wanted. "It's not up to you to decide whether to wait or not. I'm the one who will do the checking with the mud logger. Your team will need to be ready within an hour."

Then he introduced the service men to his guests. First was Sihar Situmorang, an oil analysis engineer, the man who had attracted Laila with his nonchalance and his hard physique. And his salt-and-pepper hair. The second man was also starting to go grey, but he had wicked eyes and a manner of speaking which suggested he was uneducated, at least that was how Laila interpreted it. He was Hasyim Ali, a machine operator, about seven years older than Sihar. Then there was a young man in his mid-twenties who seemed a bit nervous about his job. His name was Iman, a junior engineer working under Sihar's guidance. Rosano introduced his guests perfunctorily. "Laila, a photographer. Tony, a writer." Their meeting was a brief one.

While they were leaving, Laila noticed the man with glasses take off his singlet and use it to wipe off his sweat. He began with his neck, then his armpits, then his bare chest.

The rig was a small place. At lunchtime they met again in the mess. This time he was fully dressed in his grey overalls, trimmed at the cuffs with orange and blue stripes. Rosano called him over when he appeared in the doorway. After serving himself a generous helping of food, he brought his tray to their table. Laila watched him as he approached.

He is looking at me. This time he turns to me as I sit there next to Rosano. It is, however, the briefest of contacts. He strikes me as someone who is either painfully shy, arrogant, or utterly indifferent. He looks at my tray and says, "You're not eating much." Sihar Situmorang. And he smiles.

He had nothing more to say to her. He spoke only to Cano, about their work. He didn't look at her again, as he sat there in front of them, except when she was interrupting. She kept her eyes on him.

He spoke the flat Jakarta vernacular. But his hard Batak accent was evident from time to time, especially when he was arguing. She loved listening to it. Possibly because she was already attracted to him. Or maybe too because she was born of parents who never really liked the domineering Javanese. Her name was Laila Gagarina, a signal to any Indonesian that she was a post-1960s child of Minangkabau origins. Her father was obviously an admirer of Yuri Gagarin. Her mother was a Sundanese with ambivalent feelings about Java. Laila felt that this strong Batak accent contained a quality of honesty, of forthrightness. Or maybe she was merely projecting her own hopes onto this man to whom she was increasingly attracted. And at the table she found herself wedged between Sihar and Rosano, who were engaged in a heated exchange of opinions. Why was there so much friction between them? Sihar was constantly looking for flaws in Rosano's argument. The company man was repeatedly accusing the Seismoclypse team of running behind schedule. Laila had become so infatuated with Sihar that she found herself taking his side.

After they had eaten they each returned to their respective duties. Laila wandered around in search of an angle that would give her a distinctive shot, or one that would depict the harshness of work on the rig. But her eyes could not resist the temptation to search for Sihar. She found him and his young apprentice in front of a freight container. They were adjusting the tension on a frayed cable leading from a window in the container to the drilling well.

On the platform people in muddy clothes and uniform helmets were going about their business as if the rig were a stage and they were part of a performance. Laila photographed them at work.

"These aren't photographs for some sort of workers' campaign, are they?" Rosano greeted her in his characteristic manner – friendly, amenable, smug. Later Laila found out from Sihar that Rosano was the son of a big-shot in the Ministry of Mines and Energy. "Texcoil paid for Rosano's schooling in America and promised him a job on the proviso that his father would fast-track their tender for the concession in Natuna," he explained. But Laila didn't know if he said that out of contempt for Rosano. She was finding it difficult to be objective. She didn't really care.

She finished her work by four o'clock, a time usually marked by the call to afternoon prayer. But the summons was absent here. There was just the call of seagulls from the sky. As a girl she used to perform the five daily prayers, a marking of time by the altitude of the sun. In her mind's eye she could sense the gradient of light. Tony was still chatting. They were to spend the night on the rig because the return helicopter was being flown in from the closest island, Matak, and would not arrive until the morning. And there weren't yet regular daily flights from that tiny airport to Jakarta. They would probably have to catch a flight from another island, Natuna. But she would have had no objections at all if they had been forced to stay even longer on the rig because she had found a delicious new hobby: watching Sihar's movement back and forth into the freight container. She was reluctant to get too close to him though, because he was clearly very busy. Surreptitiously she focused her zoom lens for a nice close-up shot of him. He was reprimanding his apprentice. Grim-faced, the youth then set about repairing something.

Then she saw Rosano approaching the two men, suggesting that the problem, whatever it was, was about to continue. Straight away she could hear them arguing again, their raised voices carried to her on the wind.

"What's the story, Sihar? We need to get this job finished as soon as we can."

"We're not prepared to start yet. The risk is too high."

Rosano promptly retorted, "Let me remind you again, it is not your prerogative to decide. Contact the mud logger."

They talked by phone with the mud logger, whose job was to do the soil analysis. They argued again. "Why is it that Seismoclypse equipment can't function in high-pressure conditions like this? Other oil services can!" Rosano's voice was rising in anger. Laila watched the proceedings assiduously; this was turning into a nasty confrontation. Rosano was jabbing his finger at Sihar, who responded in kind. Laila felt herself getting tense. She could hear Sihar: "Read my lips, Cano. I won't run the equipment until the pressure has subsided."

They must have had a serious quarrel, because Sihar is no longer talking to "Mr." Rosano. This makes me feel quite uneasy because I feel certain that it will only lead to more problems. Then I hear his voice again and this time his Batak accent comes through loud and clear.

"I'll say it again, the risk is too high. *You* can cross my name off the contract if *you* insist on going ahead with the job."

He addressed Rosano with the impolite *you*.

Rosano glared at Sihar, trying to restore his self control. "Okay," he said after he had taken some deep breaths, "I'll delete your name from the contract. I will report to Seismoclypse that this was done at your own request." He turned and pointed at Iman who had been standing, transfixed, between them all the while. "You're in charge here now. Run the engine, or Seismoclypse will be up for a huge compensation bill."

Sihar, trembling slightly, chest heaving, held his anger within his jaws. He looked at his apprentice, who was speechless. The young man was overcome by the enormity of the responsibility that had suddenly been shifted to him. With his eyes he pleaded with his supervisor for mercy. Sihar could not bear to put such a huge burden on the shoulders of his assistant. Laila heard him speak again, in a milder tone, as if he were giving a little ground: "Give me a few minutes to phone the head office."

"No," Rosano grabbed the phone. "You're off the job. You've relinquished your right to give orders. You may eat and sleep on the rig if you wish, till the chopper gets here tomorrow morning. If you don't want to eat, feel free to fast." His face set in the expression of a military commander, Rosano turned to Iman again. "Run the tool!"

"You're crazy, Cano!"

Sihar ran off in search of another phone.

I don't know for sure exactly what is going on. I don't understand the finer details of their work.

Once Sihar had disappeared, the others took orders from Rosano. Hasyim wore a grim expression, as if his sympathies were still with Sihar. Nonetheless the operator went over to the mouth of the well and began the job of sending the sensor hundreds of meters down into the pit, the depth of which was supported by steel cylinders that pierced the earth's crust, the shield that preserves oil and explosive gases under extremes of high pressure. Iman barked out instructions to Hasyim who proceeded to pay out the cable the full length of the vertical tunnel. The young boy made preparations for starting up the engine. The machine began to hum.

Suddenly there was the sound of an explosion.

The platform rocked violently. Laila was thrown to her knees and was spun around for several meters. Everyone was flat to the ground. She couldn't see Sihar. What had happened?

The valves at the mouth of the well below the platform hadn't been strong enough to suppress the extraordinary power beneath it, which had suddenly surged upwards. The platform's steel base, where the workers stood, was torn apart and as the tower began to topple, three workers who had been working at the base of the rig were flung into the air like plastic toy soldiers. They did not even have time to scream. Laila had barely drawn breath when she saw the bodies of Hasyim and two others crash down onto the platform, and then skid off into the sea. Along with a sign bearing the warning *Safety first*. Earthquake. Fire. Alarm bells.

Sihar's analysis had been correct. The gas and fluid below had been so dense that they had seeped into the well and had instantly exploded with phenomenal force and speed. Everyone ran for their lives. Lifeboats and emergency capsules were at the ready but the well stabilized within a few minutes. Then Laila could hear Sihar's drawn-out curse. "Fu-u-ucked u-u-up!" He was hoarse; the curse came from the very base of his throat.

The man stands in a doorway. His eyes convey the futility of it all.

But the sea became calm again, gleaming with phosphorescence from the millions of plankton that floated near the surface. There was no sign of the three bodies. Just blood on the deck. Salt mist. Perhaps the sea was a giant liquid monster that swallowed people whole then smiled sweetly, as if it had done nothing.

Matak Island, the next day

You've hurt your hand.

At the tiny airport Sihar pounded his fist over and over into the Formica bench, chafing the tender skin of his knuckles. They oozed a dark red cherry color. The smell of salty sea air permeated the little island; there was no escape. He was furious with himself for not punching Rosano's lights out so as to prevent the accident that he predicted would happen. And now his friend was gone, his body had vanished without a trace. Rosano's only comment had been, "We regret the accident too. But they did act recklessly. And the accident was relatively minor. We didn't have to evacuate. This was a piece of good luck. This is one of the risks of the job," along with a few words of justification indicating that he considered the accident to be inconsequential. Sihar cursed himself. He felt sickened.

So Laila moved to his side. She found an excuse to sit close to him. They faced each other among an assortment of mismatched chairs. Tony and Iman sat alone, some distance from them, their faces downcast. The boy didn't speak for hours after the accident and when he did open his mouth it was to announce his resignation from Seismoclypse. This had been his first experience as an engineer, and he didn't want a second. Laila too was irate with Rosano, who had advised her and Tony not to get involved. "You came here for the sole purpose of doing the company profile that we commissioned. There's no need to transform yourself into a journalist," he had said as they waited for the helicopter to take them to Matak. She and Tony had been asking questions about how the disaster could have happened. Laila had also witnessed Rosano's final altercation with Sihar. Her attraction to him intensified her resentment towards Rosano: to her, his arrogant mouth resembled a snout photographed with a fish-eye lens that exposed his throat and the foul words in it. But before her now was Sihar's injured hand, which opened up affection between them.

"Stop it."

And he stopped.

"He was my friend. We went everywhere together."

Sihar, a man's soul is in the hands of God.

But she feared that those words would be cold comfort. And she was attracted to him. She didn't want to appear to be preaching.

"I have some Betadine. Let me clean that wound." He put his hand out and Laila washed it with bottled water and a tissue she had taken from a pack she always carried in her bag to use in toilet. She sprinkled the wound with the liquid. The tinge of brown, the glint of pavonine. The smell of iodine.

Sihar gazed towards the water as his hand was being bandaged. He had always loved the sea, but now it had swallowed his best friend and spewed out a nightmare. He feared that henceforth he would hate the sea. Later he would tell Laila about his childhood spent at seaside locations, the sound of the surf always in his ears. His father was a harbormaster. The family had moved several times, but they always lived near a port – in Gunungsitoli, Kijang, Mentok, Biliton, Sibolga. His father was from Samosir, a small island in Lake Toba, where the Batak people are considered to have the physical features that are easily stereotyped – square jaw, broad nose. His mother's ancestors were fairer, both in skin and hair. Sihar had his father's facial bone structure but his nose was finer, like his mother's. He was dark-skinned, maybe a legacy of his father or maybe a legacy of too many days outside in the sun. As a boy he had wanted to be a sailor because he couldn't be what he really wanted to be – his comic book hero "Deni the Fish-man." (He still had the comics but he had never been able to get hold of the final edition.) When he grew up he hadn't enrolled at the naval academy, because engineers were always in demand in a developing country. Engineers had more job opportunities as well. In his parents' eyes, a degree in engineering or medicine was more prestigious than any other. It was also better than being a sailor. He enrolled in the technology faculty at the Universitas Veteran Negara – people in Jakarta knew it as UPN because they pronounced "v" as "p". After he had joined Seismoclypse he once again encountered his beloved sea, his beloved islands. Many people feel stress after weeks in the middle of the ocean, but not me, he told Laila later, after they had become close. I like to stretch out on the deck before I go to bed, and for a moment look at the sea and the sky, listen to the waves and the wind. Watching the flickering of the stars and the lights from the other oil rigs in the surrounding waters. Every now and then I would watch a porn movie with my friends. Then we would usually go our separate ways and masturbate.

But that was before this. Before the sea had erased all trace of Hasyim Ali. He suddenly turned away, no longer able to derive any pleasure from watching the ripples of the waves as they pounded the sand. Hasyim Ali had worked as a machine operator, handling all the heavy work, while Sihar carried out the analyses or fine-tuned the machines. They made a good partnership and because there had never been a single problem during the time they worked together,

Seismoclypse had been sending them out as a team for the last seven years. The job was a boon for Hasyim. He was from a community of small-scale coconut farmers in South Sumatra, so with an income of around a million-and-a-half to two million rupiah a month, he was the main contributor to his family's finances.

"I feel sad too, even though I never knew him." *How dreadful for his family. Was he a faithful husband?*

Along with sixty percent of the men here, he wasn't faithful to his wife sexually. But he never neglected his family. His wife, his children, his parents and his in-laws. "I don't know who'll provide for them now."

"But there will be insurance, won't there?" *But money can never replace a human being.*

He just shrugged and they fell silent. A rumbling noise became audible in the sky. "Is that the plane coming to take you away, Sihar?" They were waiting for a chartered plane used by a number of oil companies operating in the area. They were each going in different directions. Sihar to Palembang, Laila to Jakarta. Her plane would arrive later than his, and she felt that their separation was going to happen too soon. She began to feel despondent at the thought of watching him boarding the plane, the doors shutting, the wheels being pulled up, and the aircraft leaving her sitting on an airport bench among strangers on this tiny barren island. Among the smell of shrimp paste and garlic that visitors to the island liked to take back home as gifts for their families. "No. My plane won't be here for another hour."

Suddenly Sihar began to talk again, as if his spirit had been revived.

"I have some ammunition in my bag, you know."

"What for?"

His voice was close to a whisper. "To blow Rosano's brain out."

No one can ever tell whether Sihar is serious or speaking in jest. I don't know. I can't say a thing. Explosives are of course a part of his job, used for blowing apart layers of rock. If he is serious, it is pretty careless of him to tell me, someone he's only known for half a day. But what if he actually trusts me not to do him any harm? I begin to feel uneasy at the thought that maybe he isn't joking. I don't know who he is. After all, we only met a few hours ago and it has only been in the last minutes that our conversation has assumed any intimacy. My God, what if he were to actually do it, and get caught and be sent to jail, charged with premeditated murder and possessing illegal ammunition?

"Why don't you take this case to court? Dereliction of duty resulting in a person's death is a crime."

But he gave a cynical laugh. "Don't you know who Rosano is?" It was then that he explained that Rosano's father was a high-ranking government official. "Texcoil has more than enough money to silence Hasyim's family and the police."

"Well what are you going to do then?"

"I'll blow his brains out."

Sihar, are you crazy? You're making me really nervous. Is this just his anger speaking?

"What's the harm in giving my suggestion a try? I have a friend who's a lawyer. She'll help for sure. At the very least, if we apply some pressure Texcoil will be forced to make a bigger pay-out if they want to silence people. And that will mean that Rosano is seriously out of favor with Texcoil. If he doesn't go to jail, at least he will be sacked…"

And she was relieved to see that Sihar showed some interest in her idea. This man is not crazy. He appeared to want to explore the matter a little further. He brought his face close to hers and spoke in a low voice.

But I can feel the warmth of his breath on my lips. The smell of tobacco arouses something in me. I can't put a name to it. Close up he is good-looking, like ebony or polished copper, shiny dark brown.

His eyes, disguised behind his glasses, glanced around from time to time in case anybody was listening to their conversation. But everyone else was absorbed in reading or securing their bags of garlic for their flight.

"What's your plan?"

Laila seemed to pick up on Sihar's nervousness; before replying she looked around the room full of heat-struck sleepy people. "As well as bringing Texcoil to court, the case needs to be taken up by the media. There must be people around who are willing to support the family if they are put under pressure. There must be NGOs that will protest and pursue the case. I have a friend who'll take it on."

"Who is he?"

But his question caused her to pause for a moment.

Because the man I'm referring to is from my past. Someone who had a special place in my heart when I was a teenager, then disappeared for years, and reappeared as an environmental and labour activist in South Sumatra, the place where he grew up. I idolized him when I was young. Now I probably wouldn't recognise him. It's only during the last year that he's begun to answer my letters again. We haven't seen each other since we went our own ways more than ten years ago.

"He…he's a man with lots of ideas and plenty of nerve. His name is…Saman." *His name wasn't always Saman.*

"Can you come to Palembang with me and put me in touch with these friends of yours?" Sihar asked enthusiastically, not noticing her anxiety, however fleeting.

Laila nodded. She immediately forgot her brief moment of nostalgia, because this man before her had asked her to accompany him. He went with her straight away to organize her sudden change of plans. *We won't be separating after all.*

Twelve o'clock.

I remember, after that first meeting three years ago, we had plenty of excuses to meet. From Palembang I contacted my two friends. Yasmin Moningka has never been short of male admirers, on account of her clear skin and slender figure, to the point that I was worried that Sihar would fall for her the minute he laid eyes on her. But he didn't even look at her, just as he hadn't looked at me on our first meeting, and that made me even fonder of this laid-back man. Yasmin is the smartest of my close friends, as well as being the one with the most money. We call her the girl who has everything. She's now a lawyer in her father's firm, Joshua Moningka & Partners. But she often works for a legal aid team that provides legal services for the poor and the underprivileged. She also has advocacy rights, something that not all lawyers have. As for my other friend – he's now known as Saman. He changed his name, he changed his appearance, and he now runs an NGO. He tried to re-invent himself, but I believe that essentially he's the same compassionate person as before, although his organization is considered radical. A military intelligence officer once said that his name, Saman, had a left feel about it, consisting of just two syllables like the *nom de guerre* of well-known Communists such as Lenin, Stalin, Hitler, Trotsky, Nyoto, Nyono, Aidit, (Saman) – I thought those Indonesian Communists used the names given to them by their parents. I also didn't know if Hitler was a Communist. I was never any good at history. I have no idea why my friend chose such an unfavorable name. I phoned his organization and he didn't recognise my voice at all. I wasn't upset. We hadn't seen each for maybe ten years. I felt a mix of amusement and nostalgia when I recalled how besotted I had once been with him. But that was in the past. Now my heart reaches out for Sihar.

There were many things that had to be sorted out if the case was ever going to make it to court, so the four of us had to meet frequently. But later it was more often just the two of us, Sihar and I, meeting for other reasons, and as time went by our farewells were always accompanied by a long kiss.

He had been constantly in my thoughts since the moment we met. His name had become etched into my mind as soon as Rosano uttered it to me. Sihar was a man who didn't mince his words with his superiors like Rosano, or in the workplace. But when he was with a woman he never spoke so much as a single foul word. Nor did he tell an off-color joke. There were never any lewd glances from behind the cylindrical glasses that gave him a bookish appearance. For all intents and purposes he seemed indifferent to women. Strangely, this made him more attractive, like a wild horse that doesn't care for the orderly life of the farm, which only serves to make people determined to tame it, until finally the animal begins to nibble at the clumps of hay left for him at the edge of the field.

But he was married.

A man like him should have married a nice virgin, but he married a widow with a daughter. One day in a restaurant, when we'd been meeting regularly, he confided to me about something that was bugging him. Extended Batak families expect sons, he said. I know. "Are you going to hang around until a baby boy appears?" He shook his head. "It seems that my wife can't have any more children." Then he told me about some sort of cyst that had affected her ovaries. I just said: Oh. (So he would have no descendants.)

But that day we kissed. When he took me home he said he wanted to kiss my forehead, which ended in a love bite.

Of course our relationship would give no joy to those near and dear to us. His wife and child. My parents. He would phone me with ever-changing pseudonyms. (My father was always wanting to meet the man who kept asking for me). I phoned him only at his office (at home his wife often answered). We never wrote letters, that would only provide concrete evidence for others (sometimes I actually yearned for a bit of concrete evidence that I could savor when I was alone). We would meet, have something to eat or drink, watch a movie someplace far away from his wife and my family, then kiss in the car. All the way home. But we often had to cancel our dates because his wife suddenly asked to be taken shopping or his daughter got her school report. And I would have to wait. Because I was the last on the scene. Often we would have to drive a long way out of town because he thought one of his wife's friends was nearby. But we would always part with a long kiss, him breathing harder each time. Afterwards he would usually say, "I regret the fact that I'm married. But I have responsibilities. Is what we are doing wrong? Sometimes I feel it is."

Then love became something that was wrong. Because this relationship couldn't be neatly encapsulated by something called marriage. He often felt that he was betraying his wife. It began to haunt him more and more, until one day I was so fed up on account of him repeatedly canceling dates because of his guilty feelings that I said, "Clearly you, a Batak male, are afraid of your wife." By saying this I touched a very sensitive nerve in him, because Batak culture is strongly male-oriented. "Sihar, haven't you considered the fact that I feel guilty too, towards my parents? But I've never cancelled a date with you on account of it." He was stung, and replied tauntingly, "Are you challenging me? Are you willing to let me take our relationship further?" I said nothing for a moment or two. Maybe I had been challenging his masculinity; indulging my ego's hidden desire of having him surrender before me (or making him stand erect before me, as my friend Cokorda put it). Whereas in fact I was too chicken to do more than kiss him.

So he took me to a hotel by the beach. Because it seemed that he still loved the sea. It was April 22, 1995. But that was the high point of our rendezvous. After that day I felt that he gradually began avoiding me. Until finally he thought it was best that we not see each other again. And we weren't intimate again. Perversely, I felt no hatred, rather a sense of loss of what might have been. It gnawed away at me. Because he had never violated me. He had never tried to rape me or to force me, even when we were both naked in bed. I believe that when he distanced himself from me it was simply because he could no longer restrain himself, and he wanted to protect me. He didn't want to be the one to take my virginity. I believe he still loved me and wanted me. Almost a year passed.

One day about two months ago I heard that he was going to America. I gathered my courage and dialed his number.

"I was just thinking about phoning you," his voice sounded bright.

"I hear you're off to America."

"I was going to tell you."

"What will you be doing there?"

"Seismoclypse are switching over to new technology. I've been asked to do some training in it."

"I'm going to America too. I have a friend in New York," I suddenly announced. I hadn't even thought about it, but the decision was made.

He said nothing.

"New York is a long way from Odessa, darling," he said. "About two thousand miles."

"What's that in kilometers?"

"More than three thousand, like going from Jakarta to Biak."

"Wouldn't you like to see New York?" I asked. "We could meet there."

"Wouldn't you like to see Odessa?" he asked. "We could also meet there."

But in the end we agreed to see New York before he went to

Texas. I didn't know how I could have made such an impromptu decision. Maybe I was obsessed with him, a shadow that seldom left me. Maybe I was fed up with all the obstacles to our relationship in Indonesia. Tired of the values that sometimes seemed to terrorize me. I wanted to get away from all that and allow ourselves to do the things we wanted to do. Tear away the things that had been obstructing our relationship. Maybe.

He would be leaving on May 26 but he didn't know where he would be staying. I told him I would be arriving before him. A day after he arrived we would meet on the southern side of Central Park: a piece of man-made architecture comprising trees and an artificial lake in the middle of New York City.

And that day arrived, after we'd flown thousands of miles, like the birds. This morning I'm sitting here in this open space, where humans and animals live in harmony. People are out jogging or cycling. Squirrels glide from the trees to the ground, like musk shrews, and sniff around. They gather seeds, peanuts, or cones, then scurry back to their branches. Hurry, Sihar, come and see them, they're so delicate and so alive. There are no ghetto kids around to idly shoot them with their slingshots, leaving their corpses on the side of the road, or taking them home as trophies. This is a country where city squirrels face no danger. And neither do we. See them resting there behind leaves shaped like the palm of a hand.

When Sihar gets here I'll tell him, "We can also rest here." Let's take a break from our fear and our guilt and from our families back home, like a pilgrim permitted to end his fast. Aren't you tired of being a husband? I'm tired of being scared of my father. I want to rest for a while. Isn't this park beautiful? This is the first time I've been overseas you know.

When my darling appears in that gateway, I'll tell him that it's four hundred and twenty-four days since we last met. And he'll be amazed by the fact that I've waited for him. And touched. He'll kiss my forehead. Gently, not too passionately, like someone truly in love. But I'll tell him that I'm ready this time. And I've chosen him to be my first lover. He'll ask why I chose him. I'll tell him that my friends have told me that the first time is much better with an experienced man. A virgin, they say, can't relax. He's always jittery and in a hurry.

He'll be surprised and he'll ask from where did I get this sudden boldness. Did I get that from my friends too? I'll tell him that we're like birds migrating for the mating season. I'm thirty already, Sihar. And we're in New York. Thousands of miles from Jakarta. No parents, no wife. No sin. Except in the eyes of God perhaps. But we can mate for a short time and then separate. There's nothing to regret. We love each other, don't we? Or didn't we once? Doesn't God order a man and woman to love each other when they get married? It seems not.

Then he'll say, "I've been waiting for this moment for so long," and he'll kiss me on the lips. And I'll respond so passionately that he won't be able to restrain himself any longer. Maybe we'll do it here in this park, on the bench next to the sleeping vagrant, amongst the acorns scattered by the wind. We'll do it without taking off all our clothes because it's still too cold to be naked. After that we'll do it again in the hotel room, slowly, slowly, where, without our clothes, skin can touch skin. Then, when we've finished, we'll talk. About anything at all.

After that, my darling, we'll sleep. And when we wake up we'll be so happy because clearly we will not have sinned. Even though I'll no longer be a virgin.

PERABUMULIH, 1993

When I woke up I realized I'd been asleep on his shoulder, beneath his own closed eyes. He was so tired. For a moment I forgot where we were. Our Isuzu diesel was parked in a siding off a road that cut across hectare after hectare of oil palm plantations. Rows of the palms stretched endlessly to our west, leaving an impression of a darkening mass of tightly-packed trees, their stems impossible to discern. The wind ruffled the thousands of leaves on the trees, creating a sort of Mexican wave that ebbed into the distance then flowed into the foreground. Then I remembered that we were on the way to Hasyim Ali's family home in the village of Talangrajung near Lematang river. We'd left Perabumulih at 3 AM. Sihar was exhausted because he'd had to finish a number of projects in the Seismoclypse office in Perabumulih, which had kept him up the previous night. I didn't know the way, so we had to stop. And now a sliver of dawn had awakened me with a start.

I had a dream, Sihar. We were at a party. It turned out to be our wedding. There was an ulema and a curtain. It seemed to be a secret wedding. But then, behind the curtain, at a distance but approaching me, I saw my father. Yes, it was my father hurrying towards me. Sihar was still asleep. He was exhausted.

We arrived around 10 AM at a house built of wood with a thatched palm roof. On the front verandah I saw him: Saman, whom I'd phoned from Palembang two days ago, was already sitting drinking coffee with two other men who I later found out were Hasyim's father and brother. A macaque, trained to pick coconuts, was tied to the verandah pole, screeching at them. The three men seemed to be on good terms already. I'd only just discovered that Saman had lived for a long time among these plantations. It was so long since we'd seen each other. He disappeared for several years on account of a certain incident and never replied to my letters. It had only been in the last year that our correspondence had resumed. I hardly recognized him. He was so dark-skinned and so thin, he looked like a farmer. His hair, which he used to wear shoulder-length, was now cut short. His chin was roughly shaven. I wanted to hug him for old time's sake. But something seemed to hold me back. Then I introduced Sihar to him.

The two men managed to convince Hasyim's family to take the case to court. Later, when we got home, Saman and Yasmin also persuaded the family of the other two victims to support Hasyim's family's action. The three of us returned to Perabumulih together. We were in good spirits. Sihar and Saman hit it off right away. To me they seemed to look alike, but I can't explain exactly how. Maybe it was their indifference towards women. Saman talked little about himself. He asked more about us. I told him about the accident and about the explosive Sihar was carrying to blow Rosano's brains out. I agreed that Rosano was a real troublemaker. If Cano didn't get sent to jail, maybe we should kill him, I added jocularly.

There was one thing that surprised and bothered me during the journey. When we stopped at a restaurant in Perabumulih, Saman asked me to go in first. I refused but he seemed quite insistent, saying that the two of them needed to talk privately.

"Men's business," said Saman. I was offended, but also surprised. Saman had never been like that before. In fact he'd always showed an awareness of the need to get rid of notions of men's and women's business. Had he changed? What sort of business could I possibly be excluded from? It couldn't be sex, unless Saman had done a 180 degree shift since I last saw him. Grudgingly I went into the restaurant but I chose a table from where I could keep an eye on them. They were deep in conversation. Sihar was still in the driver's seat. Saman leaned against the door. Their faces were serious for a few minutes. Their gestures suggested an argument of some sort. Clearly they weren't discussing prostitution. Then they both nodded and laughed. It was as if they were relieved that a decision had been reached. Obviously it had been a rather sensitive matter.

Suddenly it occurred to me that maybe they'd been discussing the explosives I mentioned. The world is full of people who get away with their crimes. They roam free. Some because they don't get caught, others because they are protected and can't be touched by the law. Saman had written passionately about this in a letter to me. It could well be that Rosano would be one of those who would get away with his crime. I had heard that Saman had been accused some years ago of masterminding the burning down of a factory. At the time I didn't believe it because he had always been such a noble character. But could it be true? Could it be that he was asking Sihar for his explosives so he could use them to bomb a factory in exchange for getting Rosano to court? Or could it be that Sihar was genuine about killing Rosano if the court didn't send him to jail, and he was asking Saman for help? And of course they wouldn't want to involve me in such a risky venture. Or was this all just my imagination working overtime?

As we were eating, I couldn't stop myself from asking about the ammunition. Sihar answered, "I really do want to smash Rosano's nose in. But I'm going to return the explosives. Surveillance is so tight." They didn't mention it again. But Sihar had already confided in me about his plan to keep the explosives; he would pretend to explode them in a well and then claim that they didn't go off.

We spent the next days and months organizing the case. Saman and Yasmin managed to arrange for their friends in the media to expose the issue. It wasn't easy. We suspected that in the beginning Texcoil tried to cover up the case by bribing the police and the public prosecutor not to examine it. But because the newspapers reported it constantly and because the victims' families' lawsuit was accepted by the court, Rosano was finally examined and brought to trial. Sihar was one of the most damning witnesses. But someone with influence – maybe his father and his cronies – acted as guarantor for Rosano and as a result he got a suspended sentence. He kept his job, representing Texcoil on a number of rigs as if such an accident were an everyday occurrence and an everyday occurrence were a natural thing.

Then something happened to Rosano.

When the court session had been under way for about three months, Rosano was still working on a rig at Talangatas, about fifteen kilometers north of Hasyim's family home. A tremendous commotion erupted one night when hundreds of local villagers converged upon the exploration site. They were carrying torches and oil lamps that produced huge flickering shadows on the walls, the towers and the trees. They screamed and yelled, threatening to burn the rig down if Rosano was not handed over to them. They accused him of raping a young village girl then killing her and throwing her body into a ditch that ran alongside the service road in the oil palm plantation. The corpse of a girl had been found there and there were two witnesses who had seen the girl go off with Rosano.

The siege created a major panic on the rig. Rosano yelled back that it was slander, but he was in such a state that someone else phoned for help. A helicopter from the anti-terrorist force soon arrived and evacuated Cano by air. Some of the rig staff negotiated with the irate villagers. In the end the rig wasn't burned down and the villagers dispersed after getting a guarantee that the case would be taken up by the police. They left without eliminating the company man. But the incident had a happy ending for us: Rosano lost his status as a suspended prisoner. He was sent to jail.

I kept asking Sihar and Saman what had really happened. Was Rosano really such an evil man, a rapist and a murderer? He was certainly a nasty piece of work but was he really that evil? But they just replied, "We didn't think he was either. But if it weren't the case he wouldn't have gone to jail."

But ever since their tête-à-tête while I was in the restaurant, I had felt that they were involved in some sort of conspiracy. On this occasion too I felt that they were covering something up. Maybe five or more unidentified bodies were found each week in South Sumatra. Two or three of them were women. Many of those women were raped. How difficult would it be to find a decomposing body and throw it into a ditch? How difficult would it be for a man like Saman, with his gift for winning people over easily, to convince the villagers that one of their number had been murdered by an oil rig worker who everyone already knew was a shady character? There's no way Sihar would be able to do that. But Saman could. Yet on the other hand I wasn't absolutely convinced he would be able to bring himself to do it. He used to be so gentle. He used to be so honest. Or was it that I no longer knew him since he had changed his name to Saman? Or was it all just my imagination? If so, what had really happened?

The incident left me with a disturbing sense of unease, because I didn't know whether I should be suspicious or thankful. In the end I too told myself, "I didn't believe it. But if it weren't the case he wouldn't have gone to jail."

Three o'clock.

But now the day has gone! The afternoon has passed, the beggar has disappeared and Sihar hasn't turned up. Sihar, where are you?

A feeling of doom is descending on me. I'm desolate, like that black bird, perhaps a crow, that's all alone. Where's your mate gone? Where are all the other birds that migrated for the mating season? And that creature of the night seems to be whispering in my ear: the journey, my friend, is not as wonderful as one imagines it to be. Birds have to fly without resting, fly low between the ocean and stratosphere, from continent to continent. For only from the sea can we hope for warmth, warmth that saves us from the frozen atmosphere above. Only from the sea, which provides no place to shelter. Not all of us return for the spring. Some fall to the ocean, just like man-made planes do. All of a sudden I begin to worry. I am overcome by an anxiety that makes my knees feel empty, like the shell of a snail whose flesh has been eaten away by pesticide. Did his plane arrive safely? Maybe it didn't. I need to find out, I must find out. I haven't read the paper since the day before yesterday, have I?

There's a newspaper box near the pretzel and bagel stand at the edge of the park. I run towards it with aching legs. My coins clatter down one by one as I feed them into the slot for a *USA Today*. Has there been a plane crash? Not on the front page. Nor on any of the other pages either.

But I can't feel relieved yet. I throw away the wretched newspaper. I've been in New York for a week. I haven't heard any news about Indonesia. We know that lots of things can happen in a week. A teacher kills a policeman who has accosted a *bajaj* driver, a servant is murdered for stealing a watch, a colleague is murdered and his corpse is ground into pig food! Everyone could be murdered within seven days. Sihar, I'm worried! Really worried. Are you still alive? Shortly before I left, the court ruled that Rosano was guilty. But his family is still out there aren't they? And they are powerful people. It's not inconceivable that they could undermine Hasyim's family's resolve to prosecute. They could intimidate Hasyim's wife until, in a state of fear, she blurted out Sihar's name. Not to mention the matter of the young girl who was murdered. What if, oh my God, what if they took their own revenge? We don't know what sort of people Cano's relatives are. They could hire a hit man to hide in Sihar's jeep as he was driving alone in the forest, then, when my darling was taking a rest, leap out and kill him in his sleep. Or maybe the hit man would torture him first. Then he would carelessly throw his body behind a dense clump of damp tropical ferns. Nobody would ever find it because the lichen is so moist and everything decomposes so rapidly. And the body of the man I love would lay sprawled there, like a spore fallen on fertile ground and in the space of two short weeks would be transformed into new growth. And we would never meet again. Sihar…

I have to get some news. I have to find out. From where I am standing a phone booth is visible on the other side of the two roads that loop around Columbus Circle: a circus-like microcosm that forms a tight ring around the park. Cars and trucks flash by, buses and taxis too. Everyone is self-absorbed. Some hurry along, others idly read the advertisements and neon signs. Will the light ever signal walk so I can get to that phone booth?

Green. I run.

In the booth I dial international to Jakarta, to his office. Eighteen rings. Nineteen rings…

"Can I speak to Sihar?"

"Who's speaking?"

"I'm calling from America."

"I'm sorry; it's four o'clock in the morning. Call back tomorrow. Thank you." And the line goes dead.

۞

1983. HE WASN'T USING THE NAME BACK THEN: SAMAN.

He was one of three men bathed in the light that was streaming through the three windows above the altar.

More light came in through the lead-light windows along the walls of the church. Shadows fell, stretching out from the Corinthian pillars and from the feet of the statues of the saints, pointing in seven directions. The faintest glimmer of light came from the candles that had been lit before the ordination began. The three men wore white robes, *lumen de lumine*, and the Bishop with his golden mitre called their names one by one. Among them was his name: Athanasius Wisanggeni.

The Holy Orders sacrament. The three men, barefooted, knelt and kissed the cold floor of the cathedral. They had already made their vows. They had been draped with stoles and chasubles. From that day people would be addressing them as Father. And so he became Father Wisanggeni. Or, Romo Wis, that would be the way the local people addressed him.

After the mass there was a small intimate get-together in the parish house in honour of the three new priests. The young choirboys greeted them reverentially, because every time a priest was ordained it was welcomed like a birth: there was joy, there was wonder, there was anxiety. The elderly placed their hopes, like a yoke or even a cross, over their shoulders but these new priests felt like soldiers in a legion. Their duties would be determined by the Bishop.

When he had been greeted by all the guests, Wisanggeni approached one of the senior priests present, a slightly-built man with narrow piercing eyes. This was the man he had been looking for. Between his eyes was a deeply etched U-shaped furrow, like that on the faces of ascetics in Hindu-Buddhist paintings, a sign of a holy man who was given to long periods of meditation and distanced himself from carnal matters. This was Romo Daru, an elderly priest who was known for his outspokenness in diocese meetings. But what was more important for Wis was that Romo Daru, who spent a lot of his time in the Carmelite retreat on the slopes of Mount Sindangreret, was well-known for a particular gift. The Holy Spirit had given him one of the seven gifts, namely the eyes to see through to the invisible world, and faith as robust as a mustard seed to exorcise evil spirits. Wisanggeni approached him tentatively but the old man congratulated him even before he'd had time to open his mouth. The younger man felt rather awkward and shy.

"Thank you. Do you still remember me?" They had first met about four years earlier. At that time Wis had just finished his studies in philosophy at the Driyarkara Institute of Philosophy, and was studying at Bogor Agricultural College. He had deliberately sought out this ascetic priest to tell him a strange story about his childhood, something he had never shared with anyone before, not even with his own father.

The old man nodded warmly in affirmation. "How are things? Where do you hope to be posted?"

As it happened, this was precisely the matter Wisanggeni wanted to discuss. Cautiously he told the old man of his aspirations. He hoped to be sent to Perabumulih. Why, the older man asked. I'm a graduate in agriculture, he replied. I think I could contribute a lot to a plantation area. But in that case you'd be of more service in the tiny island of Siberut, where the Catholic Church has a significant base among the nomadic people, the majority of whom still live as hunters and gatherers. Wis tried to hold his ground. I know the Perabumulih area really well, he said. When I was a boy my father often took me with him when he went out to the plantations on business. And anyway, isn't the priest there getting on in years? But Romo Daru's only response was to make brief eye contact with Wis. That was enough to change the younger man's mind about concealing his real reasons, because there had been a sub-text to their conversation.

"As you know, I have ties to the place," he acknowledged finally.

Then there was silence for a moment.

Romo Daru: "You want to go looking for something you lost a long time ago?"

"I'm also taking the news of mother's death."

"If that's the only reason, you can have a holiday there." He was gazing at the curve of the stained-glass window.

Wisanggeni fell silent. "Romo, just because I have a personal interest in the place, it doesn't mean it's not appropriate for me to work there, does it?"

"If the Bishop has other plans for you, ask for a month or two's leave in Perabumulih."

Wisanggeni desperately wanted to talk with Romo Daru about the spirits that had been in their presence, spirits that they had both felt, spirits that flew in the air or walked the earth, but Romo Daru didn't give him the time. For some reason he indicated that the conversation was over.

When night had fallen Wisanggeni propped himself up on his bedhead. Beyond his bedroom door the lights had been turned off in the corridor. From time to time he heard the squeak of a door and footsteps as someone went to the bathroom. His own bedroom light was still on. He could hear the silence even as the vibrations of the fluorescent tube reverberated in his eardrums. There was also the sound of a tap dripping in a far-off toilet. He gazed at the photo of his mother on the bedside table. Mother. "My mother."

PERABUMULIH 1962

Perhaps he was lucky. He was the only child born from his mother's womb who had survived. Two of his younger siblings had never been born; one had died at the age of three days.

His mother, a Javanese woman of noble origin, was a figure who could not always be described in rational terms. She often seemed not to be in places she was or to be in places she wasn't. At such moments it was difficult to engage her in conversation because she didn't listen to people around her. Sometimes her silence would be brought to an end by a visit to a place that nobody knew, a space that didn't exist anywhere: an emptiness. But when she was present in the place she occupied, she was very warm and affectionate and her husband and other people would forget about the other incomprehensible side of her nature. In bed she would listen to her husband as he lay with his head on her soft bosom, talking endlessly in a voice that sounded like a buzz in the middle of the night, and resonated through the air vents above the door. In the mornings she would sing Javanese rhymes about the orioles for the young Wis, as well as for the neighbor's children and for the birds and animals in the vicinity. Wis would curl up in her lap like a suckling kitten. When she was present in the place she occupied, where you could see her, she was like the sun. The planets would be drawn into her orbit and would circle her in safety. That was how Wis remembered his mother.

His father had no noble blood in his veins. Like other common people in Java at that time, his parents gave him only a nickname and, as was common practice at that time, he chose his own name in adulthood. He had taken on the name Sudoyo. He was from Muntilan and was devoutly religious, unlike Wis's mother who, although she went to church on Sundays, also revered the *keris* and other sacred heirlooms. Sudoyo was the son of a medical aide. He had worked for a bank in Yogyakarta ever since he was an economics student at Gajah Mada University. Wisanggeni was born there. When he was four years old his father was transferred to Perabumulih, a town on another island, whose main road was only about five kilometers long.

At that time Perabumulih was still a quiet oil town in the middle of South Sumatra. There was only one cinema, so people were in the habit of taking their children on outings to the rig outside town, to watch the oil-scooping machine nodding its head about like a dinosaur. The other sources of entertainment were the *lutung*, the long-tailed monkeys, and the gibbons, that would suddenly leap from the trees. The bank hadn't been there for long. His father was the branch manager. They lived on the top floor of a reasonably spacious wood frame house almost at the end of Kerinci road, the town's main street. The ground floor served as the office. Besides the bank clerks who were there during working hours, there was one servant in the house. Somir, that was what Wis's father called the young man.

Behind the house was a garden that bordered on a big area of forest that got denser and denser as it receded into the distance. Father would not allow Wis to venture too far into the forest. Are there ghosts? he asked. No, Father replied. There's something scarier than ghosts: snakes. The Devil. Lucifer. Beelzebub. Leviathan, slithering snakes, sliding snakes. A long time ago the serpent coaxed Eve into eating fruit from the tree of knowledge, which God had forbidden. Mankind fell into sin. That marked the beginning of our enmity towards the servile creatures that were cursed by God to a fate of slithering on their stomachs in order to get around. And there are a hundred snakes in that forest. The python will squeeze your sweet neck. The viper sprays poison from its mouth. The *anang* snake lives at the edges of the yard and will bite you even in the daytime. When night falls the cobra lies in wait. And the *bungka* snakes hide beneath fallen logs. Their poison destroys your nerves or freezes your blood. You'll go mad and die. And from the gnarled branches of a big tree, covered with parasitic plants and wild orchids of white and purple, a giant python watches. Maybe a pair of them, male and female. As quick as a flash its tail will wrap itself around your torso and its jaw will seize your head, then it will suck your whole body into its tunnel-like gullet towards the darkness. Its powerful ribs will crush all your bones so that your body will be as soft as a worm, your skin intact but your insides pulverized. It's the most dangerous of all. When a poisonous snake attacks you, it's because it feels threatened, but a python preys on humans because it's hungry. And a poisonous snake will leave the corpse of its victim behind, but a python leaves nothing. And your small body won't be enough to satisfy its hunger.

So Wisanggeni never ventured beyond the brush fence that his father had put up at the back of the garden. He just played in the yard that they'd planted out with cassava and vegetables. There were clumps of sugarcane, too, in the corners. When the knuckled stems of the sugarcane were mature and the color of ash, and before they flowered, Mother and Somir would harvest several and cut them into small squares. Wis would suck on them eagerly, as a substitute for sweets, until not a drop of liquid remained. While his father was at work in the front part of the house, Wis and his mother could often be found resting on the back terrace, looking out towards the trees that got denser and denser as they receded into the distance.

The closest ones were clumps of banana palms and bamboo that were so old they formed a canopy. When you got close to them it became apparent that the sheath on the knuckles of the bamboo was another world where ants and white lice lived, sheltered from the sun and the tropical rain. Next were the coconut palms, both the tall variety and the early-ripening kind, whose flowers and shoots provided food for the rhinos. Then came the fruit trees: durian, jackfruit, longans. And behind all those were the trees that developed sturdier and sturdier trunks and broader and longer branches with age, and became harder and harder to identify. But Mother seemed to know them all personally, from afar. Once she had pointed out a tree, she would never forget it. "See that tree over there?" her hand pointing in a north-easterly direction. "There's a monkey with her baby nestled in its branches." They would hear the squealing that echoed until it seemed that there were hundreds of monkeys. The next day Wis would ask again which tree was home to the monkey and her baby. "That one," Mother would point in the same direction. "The one with the dark foliage. From this angle it's directly behind that coconut palm. If you move that way a bit, it's directly to the left of the palmyra palm." To Wis, there were dozen of coconut trees and palmyras and hundreds of dark shadows. He couldn't tell one from another. But he believed his mother could. Wis believed that if his mother went into the forest (which she may well have done) then she would not get lost. But Mother warned him not to go playing too far in. "Because there are a hundred snakes in there?" he asked. "No," said his mother. "Because spirits and fairies live there." "What are they like?" "They're a lot like us." But Wis didn't see anything.

One day Father seemed happy on account of Mother feeling nauseous. You're going to have a little brother or sister, said his father. In your mother's stomach there's a baby that's still soft, that breathes through the foetal membrane, that feeds through the umbilical cord attached to its intestine because it doesn't have any teeth yet. The only baby Wis had ever seen was a kitten which was also very soft and which gave off a special smell that was a mixture of stale milk and baby poo that was so delicate that it barely left a trace. Father and Mother said that having a baby was a joyful thing, and Wis would gaze at his mother in amazement, as her stomach and breasts got bigger by the day. His mother looked more beautiful than ever, but she became increasingly contemplative and retreated more and more often into her daydream, the emptiness.

Then something happened.

When his mother came home from wherever she'd been she wasn't pregnant any more. Her stomach was no longer distended. She looked exhausted. She threw herself onto the divan on the back terrace and looked at the trees, which got denser and denser as they receded into the distance. Wis didn't know exactly what had happened but he felt that something had. He went to get his father from his office. Then the man rushed to be with his wife, whose stomach was now flat. Where's our baby? But his wife was in a dream. *Man comes from nothing and returns to nothing. Man comes from emptiness and returns to emptiness.* That day Sudoyo took his wife to the hospital, a clinic owned by the state oil company Pertamina. The doctor and the midwife said that there was no longer a baby in her womb. But neither was there any bleeding. How far gone was she? Six or seven months, said Sudoyo. Maybe it was a phantom pregnancy? A miscarriage? But where had the baby fallen? Where was the blood? In the forest?

Sudoyo sought the help of all his friends and neighbors in looking for a baby that had fallen in the forest. But nobody found it.

"Father, father, maybe it was eaten by a python?" said Wisanggeni.

That week too the husband requested a requiem mass for his lost baby. Since then he had employed a maid to look after Mother. Aunt Dirah was from Java. Wis called her Lik Dirah, and his parents would use the same term of address as the child. She was a distant relative of Father's, from a poor uneducated family, some of whom worked as servants or agricultural labourers. Her son was studying to be a mechanic, Father supported him financially.

Four months later Mother was pregnant again. Sudoyo told Lik Dirah repeatedly that his wife was not to go anywhere alone. He coaxed his wife not to become pensive, and especially not to wander into the forest with an empty soul. Recite the rosaries as much as possible, and the litanies too. One month passed, two, three. The midwife declared that the pregnancy was normal. After the fifth month the same thing happened. But Mother had not gone back to the forest. That day Mother just lay on her bed. I want to rest by myself, she had told Lik Dirah. The old woman then did some cooking in the kitchen and took lunch to Sudoyo in the office. Somir collected Wis from school, five hundred meters down the road. When Wis got off the bike beside the house he heard the cries of a baby from the window of his mother's room on the second floor. He turned towards the direction of the sound and listened hard. That was the first time he ever heard a baby cry, in that high-pitched staccato way. He could faintly hear his mother singing a Javanese rhyme, a rhyme that always brought peace to Wis's heart: *lela lela ledhong...* How was Mother after giving birth to his little brother or sister? What was the baby like and where had it come from?

But Somir just adjusted the chain of the bike. Over by the well Lik Dirah was scrubbing the blackened bottom of a pan with ash and coconut fiber. Father was still in the office. Nobody was paying any attention to Wis's high spirits.

"Is it a boy or a girl?"

Nobody answered.

"Somir! Is it a boy or a girl?"

The young man turned around. "Do you want a brother or a sister?"

"I don't know. Come on, let's go and see it." Jumping up and down, he tugged at Somir's hand.

He bounded up the wooden stairs and opened the door to Mother's room.

But the room fell silent as soon as the door opened. There was no baby; its crying could no longer be heard. There was just silence, and Mother lying on the iron-frame bed. She had fallen asleep with a relieved smile on her face and covered in perspiration that made her sarong cling to her body, so they could see her stomach that was no longer swollen. But there was no baby in the room, which was lit up by the late morning sunshine that penetrated the curtains. Just silence. And then the sound of Somir screaming. Panic-stricken, he summoned Father and Lik Dirah. The doctor was called and Sudoyo got the same answer: there was no longer a baby in his wife's womb. It had vanished without leaving a trace of blood, as if it had been absorbed into the atmosphere. From the conversation of the stunned adults who were in a state of complete shock, Wis gathered that nobody else had heard the baby crying. Nobody else had heard that the baby had been born. But something held him back from telling them.

The family held a funeral mass, and his mother joined in the procession like a repentant sinner. Tears streaming down her face, over and over again she kissed the hand of her husband whose love for her had not waned even though she never told him what had happened. But people began to believe that the babies had been taken by the spirits that lived nearby. Some of Sudoyo's friends suggested he call in a sage to exorcise the harmful spirits and ghosts, which may have been sent by someone with a grudge against him. He always refused because he didn't believe in superstition. Even though the doctors were at a loss to explain what had happened, Sudoyo regarded it as an aberration in the human body. When his employees offered to find a medicine man for him, he just politely declined. You see, I believe only in God Almighty and the power of prayer.

It was the second time they had held a funeral Mass without a body.

After the mass Somir accompanied the priest home. Father returned to his desk to tidy up the paperwork which had been interrupted because of what had happened. He had already asked Wis and Lik Dirah to go with Mother to her room. The bedroom was quite spacious, about six by six meters. The duck egg blue iron-frame bed where Father and Mother slept abutted the right-hand side wall. To the left they laid out a mattress on the floor for Wis and Lik Dirah because Father didn't want Mother to be left alone. Wis lay facing the left-hand wall. It was hot. Lik Dirah fanned him until he fell asleep.

But at midnight he awoke with a start because the baby was crying in the bed. Then he heard Mother wake up as she talked to her hungry baby. The bed squeaked as she positioned herself to feed the baby. She sang a lullaby in her gentle voice: *lela lela ledhong.*

Wis bolt upright and looked behind him, towards the bed. But the voice disappeared as soon as he saw his mother sitting up on her mattress. A dim lamp illuminated her face, which was relaxed and smiling. Wis seemed to have been woken up from a dream. He looked at the old woman next him. Lik Dirah was sound asleep. Her mouth was open and she was snoring gently. She clearly hadn't heard a thing. Father was still downstairs. Wis was a bit confused, but he lay back down again.

When his eyes were heavy and he was on the verge of sleep,

the sound came back. From behind him, from the direction of the bed. At first it was blurry because of a buzzing noise that then diminished. Whatever was going on at the back of his neck felt real to him. Mother was trying to pacify her whimpering baby. Then there was a man's voice, suddenly right there in the room. He was talking to Mother, but Wis couldn't understand the language they were speaking. He just picked up the intonation that reverberated in a calm wave, like the breeze that was blowing that evening. They seemed to be blissfully watching over the baby. The man was listening to Mother as she intoned: *lela lela ledhong*. The man wasn't Father.

Wis's head jerked around, from fear and from shock. But once again the voices disappeared the moment he turned. The dream attached itself to the back of his head; his eyes could never reach that particular wavelength. All he could see was his mother, stretched out on the bed.

"Mother!"

She was silent. Like when she was in a place she wasn't.

"Mother!"

After he had called her name several times without getting a response, Wis got up and went out of the room. His mother remained undisturbed, like a stone statue in an ancient temple. Wis descended the unlit staircase, anxiously seeking his father in the downstairs room. He found him still at work, with the base of the globe on his reading lamp starting to go black, indicating it was almost extinguished. His father turned. What is it, son? And Wis felt a surge of relief. Suddenly he yearned for his father's affection. Sobbing, he embraced him. What's the matter, son? But Wis still couldn't tell his father about what he'd experienced. He never could. It was only eleven PM.

The incidents were gradually forgotten, because for the next three years mother didn't fall pregnant again. But Wis still regularly received the visitations. The voices of young children and a man at the back of the nape of his neck, an independently-existing realm behind his own face. If the voices ever came towards him, then they would be emanating from another room. They would come at any time of day, morning, noon or night. Gradually Wis became accustomed to his mother's secret visitors, the children and the man his father knew nothing about. Whose bodies he had never seen. Let alone their faces.

Wis never heard his father complain. He kept on with his job, never asking his boss for a transfer so that they could remove themselves from the mysterious and upsetting events that had enveloped their lives. He prayed without caring whether or not God would answer his prayers. He never pried into his wife's behavior. For her he had nothing but love.

Three years went by and mother was pregnant again. This time Sudoyo began to feel the effects of anxiety. He considered sending his wife back to Yogyakarta until the birth of their baby. Her family agreed to the idea. But she herself said, "Do you want the baby to be born without seeing its father?" In the end Sudoyo asked his mother-in-law to come to Perabumulih to be on guard, taking it in turns with Lik Dirah, so that his wife wouldn't be left alone for a second. Even when she went to the toilet. The house took on an air of excited tension. Grandmother made a special brew from coconut oil, which Mother drank to ensure a smooth birth. Lik Dirah boiled up mung beans so the baby would have a thick head of hair.

Then came the time for the birth. The whole family was ecstatic. Sudoyo had taken leave and insisted on being in the birthing room, praying constantly as a way of calming his heart that was beating faster than it ever had in his life. He sat beside his wife who lay with legs apart as the contractions began. Her breathing was being monitored by the midwives. The doctor broke the fetal membrane and the head appeared a few moments later. A girl. Crying lustily.

Sudoyo wept, tears trickling from the corners of his eyes, as they did when he muffled his cries during orgasm. It was an overwhelming relief.

On the third day Sudoyo brought the baby home, where it was easier for his mother-in-law to watch over and care for her daughter and grandchild. Neighbors and friends came to offer congratulations and gifts: fruit, baby clothes, warm blankets, diapers. They chatted until late at night and when they went home they left behind silence and a floor littered with little piles of peanut shells. And cups containing tea and coffee dregs. But the family was so happy that they decided to leave the cleaning till the next day. Lik Dirah and Somir were given permission to go to bed straight away because they were both exhausted from the excitement of the day.

But night fell with a vengeance.

Once he was satisfied that his wife and baby were sound asleep, Sudoyo went downstairs to catch up on some work. Wis, Mother, grandmother and the baby all slept in the same room. They slept until once again Wisanggeni awoke with a start. It was around one AM. He was woken by the hair at the nape of his neck, which was standing on end. The skin on his neck and shoulders was like gooseflesh, as if it had come into contact with something cold. The fine hairs were like a cat's fur when it's about to pounce, receptive to the slightest touch, and alerting it of danger during its first tentative movements. He heard footsteps. Still a long way off, coming from the forest, on ground made muddy by recent rain. The footsteps were approaching the house. Wis's whole being was suffused by an overpowering anxiety, which he absorbed from the air through the pores of the skin at the nape of his neck and which then spread through his bloodstream to his arteries and heart. He sat bolt upright on his mattress and looked at his sleeping mother and grandmother. And at his ruddy-skinned baby sister. His mother was grimacing as if she were having a bad dream. But Wis's first thought was for his father. Since Mother had lost the second baby, since he had sensed the presence of his mother's visitor, Wis had become closer to his father. That was the reason he immediately thought of his father working downstairs in his study. Sensing danger, he bounded down the stairs. The tears were welling in his reddened eyes.

He called out, "Father? Father?"

He saw him with his head on the desk. Wis screamed.

His father woke up. What's the matter, son? Wis just sobbed and begged to be hugged.

A few minutes later his sister's crying was audible. And this is what grandmother later told them:

She was woken by the lusty cries of her newborn granddaughter. But she could see the baby's mother sleeping, motionless. Probably exhausted. She tried to get up to see if the baby's diaper needed changing. But she felt something nailing her body to the mattress, it seemed to be crushing her: she was in that void between sleep and consciousness, where the imagination runs wild like a dream but the senses tell you it's really happening, where the brain is functioning but is incapable of instructing the nerves to activate the body. She strained and struggled. Using all the power she could muster, she finally managed to sit up. But something struck her on the chest and she fell to the floor. Then the baby stopped crying.

The baby's breathing stopped too, as it had when Wis and Father found her.

Mother didn't wake up until her husband broke down the door, because for some reason it was difficult to open from outside. She was wide-eyed and weeping, like someone who has woken from a nightmare only to discover that it wasn't a dream at all. Grandmother was still curled up on the floor. Wis was lost for words because he could still hear the baby's crying at the back of the base of his skull. And he was so afraid. Because his sister was still alive even though she was dead. Because his mother had let it happen. Because he had felt that there was something else so close to Mother, something with which she was united, something so loving. And he suddenly felt so sorry for his father. He went up to his mother. He hit her in tears of rage, until father grabbed him from behind. Wis hadn't wept like this since the day he was born.

All that night Sudoyo held his wife to his chest. Sweat poured out of him like drops of blood. The third mass was held once the family had watched over the dead baby for a full day and a full night. This was the first time they had held a requiem mass with a body, which they put in a tiny coffin on the dresser, a little wooden box like an old-fashioned European music box, which they then took to the cemetery in a black car, to be buried deep in the earth.

Requiem. Requiem aeternam.
In paradisum deducant te angeli.

TWENTY-TWO YEARS LATER

1984. Finally he made the journey. By then he was twenty-six. He'd gone by ferry, jam-packed with passengers and vehicles, across the Sunda Strait from Merak to Bakauheni, and then he'd taken the train north. He got off at Perabumulih.

Maybe God had sent him. Maybe He had simply granted him his wish. The bishop appointed him as the priest of the Parid parish, which served the small settlements of Perabumulih and Karang Endah in the Palembang diocese. There were only around five hundred parishioners in the diocese. Perhaps Romo Daru had put in a good word for him (Wis hadn't been able to contact him to find out or to thank him), so he could find the things he'd lost, the things he'd left behind ten years earlier, when his father had been transferred to Jakarta. Wis still recalled the way his mother had wept like a widow who has lost her only child. She wept silently, because her voice was gone, but her breath and her body quivered, her teeth chattered. Mother didn't say a word, she made no signs of protest, she didn't complain, she just trembled. By that time Wis was old enough to understand intuitively that the departure was putting distance between his mother and something that she loved, something that loved her as well. Now that he had matured and his jealousy and anger had ebbed away, now that his mother was dead, Wis understood how painful that separation had been for her.

But there were still many things he had to do in order to quell his feelings of anxiety about that house, where his mother had given birth to his younger siblings. The name of the street had changed, from Kerinci to Sudirman, from the name of a mountain in Sumatra to that of a Javanese general. The parish was thirty kilometers out of town in Tasik Road, on the way to Palembang. But there was a church that had been built by the state oil company and that was shared with the Protestants. Wis usually went there on his motorbike. In addition to his parish duties he set up his own schedule for visiting old family acquaintances. It wasn't only for the sake of reaffirming the relationships, but also because he needed them to re-establish a mental map of the area, much of which he'd forgotten in the intervening ten years – even though Perabumulih hadn't changed much. Their former servant, Somir, had left the district and nobody knew where he was. Wis was deeply disappointed about that, because he would have certainly had a lot to say. But a number of other acquaintances were still around. Sarbini, who used to be in charge of Bimas, the government credit scheme, was now a businessman and middleman. Kong Tek – as he used to call the Chinese man who had owned a *warung* near their home – had changed his name to Teki Kosasih because recently the Chinese were encouraged to change their names to ones that sounded more Indonesian, and was a supplier for an oil company. His business was flourishing. Wis found out from him that their old house was no longer used by the bank. It was currently being used by a mining company as the home for the area manager. Wis often went past the house and he would always look at it with a knot in the pit of his stomach. The wood-frame house stood there as before, but the sign out the front – that he used to climb on – was gone. The gate to the house was shut and locked like that of a normal house.

When, with some hesitation, he finally went to the house, a young pregnant woman opened the door. Wis was startled; he hadn't prepared himself for encountering a stranger in his childhood home. And she was heavily pregnant too, like Mother had been when they lived there. He was speechless for a few moments.

"Excuse me for calling so early in the day," he said nervously. The house seemed empty, and the woman wasn't keen on inviting a stranger in. "I'm the new priest here. But I'm not here to talk about religion. I just wanted to have a look around. I lived here as a child. For about ten years." Then they continued their conversation on the doorstep, Wis maintaining a very formal demeanor. When they had said their farewells he asked if it would be all right if he came back when the woman's husband was at home. Her name was Asti, or Astuti, he hadn't paid that much attention. Because the woman's pregnancy made him nervous, he didn't dare to ask.

He met her husband the second time he went there, on the *Nyepi* holiday. And he was relieved that the man bore absolutely no resemblance to his father. He was tall, with light-colored skin and Arab features. His name was Ichsan, or Ichwan, again he hadn't paid that much attention. They were a polite, kind couple. They were really pleased to be able to give back the joys of childhood to someone, a guest they didn't know, by allowing him to return to his past. But for Wis the opportunity wasn't quite so joyful. He was overwhelmed by nostalgia at the smell of timber which sucked him back to his childhood. He could see himself as a child running up the stairs to their rooms on the upper floor. Then going down to the back verandah that faced the forest, growing more and more dense as it receded into the distance. "Can you still hear the monkeys?" he asked. "Occasionally," they replied. Then Wis told them about the monkeys that often used to come down from the branches and from behind the foliage and scoot over to the children visiting the oil refinery. The children would be terrified and would scramble back to the car. "Oh yes, we often see the monkeys out at the refinery," said the husband. "Black, with feet like hands. They're not like other animals, four-legged. These monkeys are four-handed." Wis was actually thinking about the footsteps he used to hear coming from the forest. And the sound of children's laughter. Where were those voices now? Would I still have been able to hear them once Mother had gone? Would they still be the once-familiar voices of children? "We are expecting our first child," said Ichwan excitedly. Wis was nonplussed: "Don't have it here!"

"Of course we're not having it here."

"Why?" (He felt foolish asking such a silly question.)

"Well, the company's paying. So why not go to Jakarta to have it?" Ichwan was still bubbling with excitement. "So my dear one can be near her family."

Wis felt a sense of relief.

They became good friends. Wis would drop in at the house whenever he was free at a suitable time, but he never let on what it was that compelled him to keep returning. Two months before her baby was due Asti went home to Jakarta. It was only then that Wis told Ichwan about his youngest sister, the one who had lived for just three days. They both concluded that it was probably because of inadequate hygiene in the local clinic. He kept to himself the story about the two babies that vanished in the womb. Ichwan joined his wife a week before the birth. The man trusted Wis so much that he kindly gave him the key to the house so he could continue to relive his childhood memories. The only other person who had a key was Ichwan's driver, Rogam.

One evening he dropped by the house on his way home after giving the final sacrament to the victim of a car accident. Rogam had gone home; he usually left in time for evening prayer. Wis switched on the lamp in the corner of the room where his father's desk used to sit and which was now occupied by a chair and a telephone table. He sat down on the chair and read. But the words in the newspaper only opened up more avenues to memories of the house. Every now and then he folded up the paper in order to pray, not knowing whether what he was uttering was a prayer or his tentative hope that he might come in contact with the voices again. If the prayer were to be answered it would provide solace for nobody but himself. Could such a request properly be called a prayer? Was it acceptable for him to ask God to allay his own personal anxiety? He went back to his reading but just kept looking at the same paragraph over and over. Finally he decided to go back to the parish. It was only seven thirty.

When the lamp had been switched off, he felt something. Not a voice, not a noise either, but rather the sensory perception that there was someone else in the room, close to him. His reflexes sprang into action; his fingers flicked the light switch on again. But in the light he saw nobody. He thanked God that it wasn't a burglar or a thief. But his heart was in his mouth. Am I afraid? Maybe he was distressed on account of his hopes, on account of the things that he'd experienced, and because he didn't know what might happen in a moment's time, or indeed because nothing at all might happen. But the sensation was becoming increasingly acute. There was somebody in the atmosphere of the room; somebody had come in on the molecules of the breeze. Wis immersed himself in the sensation. From behind he began to hear voices, a woman, occasionally a man, more often a woman, speaking in a language he couldn't understand, but nonetheless he felt that they were addressing him. Wis turned around swiftly, as if he hoped somehow to apprehend the voices with his eyes. He didn't see a thing. The voices were still there at the base of his skull, breathing warmly onto his neck and shoulders, making his skin creep. "Are you my little sister...?" Wis spoke in a strained tone, somewhere between a question and a statement. *The Lord is my Shepherd, I shall not want.*

His heart was pounding. He could still hear the strange voices from near his back. He turned off the lamp, closed his eyes and surrendered himself and his fear to a realm that seemed to be calling him from behind, a realm that he had been strangely longing for for more than ten years. "Mother died of uterine cancer," he said softly. "She missed you a great deal, I know." And the voices seemed to respond, not in any language he had ever studied, but at one point he felt that he could understand them. There were three of them. They were adults, like him. Wis was amazed that he could understand what they were saying, things that earlier he had not been able to fathom at all. He opened his eyes slowly, making sure that his consciousness remained on the wavelength where he could communicate with the voices. "Sister? What do you look like?" Again he summoned up the courage to turn around. Still he saw nothing. He turned back. And still encountered nobody. But on the northern wall of the room hung a mirror in which, if he moved over a little, he could see his reflection. Instinctively he went up to it, seeking both his own reflection and those of the people behind him.

The mirror faced the window. The window was open. What do you look like?

He saw himself reflected in the glass. There was nobody at the base of his skull. But in the dim light outside he could see someone staring into the room through the open window. Wis focused hard on the figure. What was it? It had a red seal on its brow – maybe stamped there by some subterranean beast, or by the horsemen of Gog of Magog from Meshech and Tubal, in their coats of armor the color of blue flame and sulfur. And the seal was the number six hundred and sixty-six. 666. Could this be some godforsaken creature bathed in sulfur by Satan and released from a thousand years imprisonment in the valley of death? That might explain why one of its bulging eyes looked ready to pop out of its head and the other sank back into its cheek. Its mouth gaped open and its tongue flickered like a lizard's.

Wis could barely breathe. He was unable to move.

Both eyes of this creature, those two mismatched eyes, gazed at him intently, observing him with its head erect like a reptile ready to attack. Then it smiled. It emitted a sort of staccato moan. It was the voice of a woman, its hand was waving. Calling me? But that wasn't the voice that he had heard earlier. He only then became aware that his back was pushed hard into the timber wall, which felt warm against his cold clammy fingers. The creature smiled again. This time it was like a friendly laugh, like an innocent creature cursed by God, like the prophet Job who was afflicted by disease though he'd committed no sin, or like the first-born children who came into the world as Egyptians when God was siding with the children of Israel. Wis's fear slowly transformed itself into compassion. "Are you...my sister?"

It moaned again, it seemed to be saying "what" or "who". Its words were created in a flat monotone.

Hesitantly, and rigid with fear, Wis approached this creature who had been watching him all the while. He stopped about a meter from the window. He saw that it was a girl. She was hideous-looking, but Wis could see the outline of her breasts beneath her scabby singlet. She had childlike features. Her skull was flat and her nose was small. Her mouth seemed unable to close, like that of a constantly hungry baby. How old could she be? Fifteen perhaps. But she was like a five year old with a speech impediment. "Who are you? What's your name?" he asked, perturbed. The girl replied in her own language. Wis didn't understand but he was convinced that the child was harmless. Poor thing.

He moved closer. He smiled. He felt sorry for her.

But suddenly the girl's hand darted out and grabbed him by the throat.

The creature seemed ready to devour him. Her mouth, which earlier had seemed so childlike, was now clearly full of razor-sharp teeth, like a piranha's, exposing a throat that looked set to suck in its victim's eyes and nose. Wis's reflexes sprang into action, he slapped her hand and pushed her hard. The girl fell to the gravel from the force of the blow. The air was filled with the sounds of her moans and sobs. The young man peered out of the window and regretted his panic, although it had all happened so quickly. "I'm sorry...I'm sorry," he said over and over again, as he jumped out of the window to help her. He glimpsed the expression of fear on her face as she suddenly leapt up and ran towards the forest, the forest that got more and more dense the further you ventured into it, the home of evil spirits and fairies, and of thousands of fierce snakes of a hundred varieties. Don't! Don't go too far into the forest! It's night time already.

Wis managed to grab the girl's arm, but she struggled violently. Her screams were becoming so forceful that Wis let her go because he feared that people might think he was trying to rape a young girl. And she was defenseless, handicapped. She just kept running. In the darkness, about fifteen meters in front of him, Wis saw her suddenly get swallowed up by the earth. She just disappeared into the ground and vanished without a trace, leaving Wis utterly dumbfounded. What's been happening to me? Could it be Satan who has been taunting me with these hallucinations?

But he could faintly hear a sound from the spot where the girl had disappeared. A long whine, with rounded vowels and nasal diphthongs. Wasn't it a cry for help? Or was this a trap set by the evil spirits? Whatever the case, the voice lured him towards it. Mesmerized, Wis moved towards the sound. He was terrified. A few moments later he came across a well, from whence came the cries. But the girl was nowhere to be seen because it was so dark and because the opening of the well was long and narrow. He felt completely helpless and had no idea what he should do; for a moment he wasn't sure what was happening. Eventually he shouted for help, as he ran to the back door of the nearest neighbor's house. "Help! A girl has fallen into the well!"

Half a dozen men responded to his call. Then some women came with torches, kerosene lanterns and candles. A coil of rope too. They gathered around the dark hole, flashing their lights downwards, and the shadows they cast on the hollows of their cheeks, their noses and their eye sockets gave them the appearance of Balinese *barong* dancers having a party around the campfire. The girl's voice was no longer audible. The well is dried up, someone said. It is very deep. A child fell down three years ago. He died, along with someone who went down on a rope to rescue him. There is poisonous gas in there, hydrogen sulphide. If the level gets high enough it can kill you in a matter of minutes. Who was it who fell? A girl, she seemed to have some sort of speech impediment. "Oh her, the mad one," someone said. "Her? Oh dear, what a shame..." said one of the women. "So you know her?" asked Wis, relieved, but also disquieted because these people seemed to be gradually coming to some sort of a decision. Now that they knew who she was they seemed rather reluctant to do anything.

Wis asked for a scarf to cover his nose and mouth. "Tie the rope around me." He also told one of them to go after Rogam, who he was sure would be able to lay his hands on a gas mask like the ones miners used. After they had tied the rope around his waist and shoulders they eased him off the rim of the well, along with another coil of rope. Wis made his way down the wall of the abandoned well, which had dried up long ago. He flashed his torch towards the bottom of the well. He spoke little, in order to save oxygen. As he descended he felt his chest become tighter. About twenty meters down he came across the girl, curled up in the fetal position. He was feeling quite weak himself. Hastily he took the second rope and made a slip-knot seat for the girl. He signalled to the people above to pull them up. But then he dropped his torch. Wis had lost consciousness.

Wisanggeni was awakened by familiar voices.

But when he opened his eyes, the only person he could see was Rogam, sitting beside his hospital cot. Where was the girl? She was still unconscious in the next bed. In the following days people told of how Wis and the girl were as light as feathers when they were pulled from the well, as if they were being lifted by some supernatural force. Wis kept this mystery to himself.

As he lay there in the dimly-lit hospital ward he observed the creature that had startled him in the dark. She was certainly no beauty, although she wasn't as hideous as he had first thought, in his state of shock. Her face was asymmetrical. The skin of her cheek was soft; she must be still in her teens. There was the odd pimple here and there on her face. But her skull; there was no doubt that her skull carried only a small volume of brain. Her low forehead was stained red from a weeping wound, which had been infected for a long time. And now she had a broken leg, which the doctor had set in a plaster cast.

"Who is she?"

"The daughter of one of the transmigrant families in Sei Kumbang. She used to hang around here quite a bit. She's a bit...

you know..." Rogam circled his fingers in the air around his head.

Wis looked at the girl uneasily. Rogam continued his story. Nobody knew her name. People called her whatever they liked: Eti, Ance, Yanti, Meri, Susi, anything. Like a dog in need of affection, she would respond to any name ending in "i": Pleki, Boni, Dogi. She had achieved notoriety in this town for one thing. She was in the habit of wandering around the streets and rubbing her genitals against any suitable object – a post, a fence, the corner of a wall – like an animal in heat. Of course a number of the local boys had taken advantage of this particular habit of hers. Everyone said she enjoyed it too. That's why she keeps coming back to town, they said, in search of an electricity pole or a man. And she would always be certain to find both: a passive pole and an aggressive man. "But everyone says she's mad," Wis whispered in bewilderment. Rogam chortled. He said: even a hole in the wall can give you pleasure, if it's made of flesh it's even better. Wis said nothing. He had never had sex. Rogam wasn't aware of that.

The hospital personnel were reluctant to keep the girl in for long, because there was nobody who could pay for her treatment. So they took her home in Ichwan's company jeep. She was still very weak and slept for the duration of the journey. The four-wheel drive Trooper sped southwards on the winding road, passing watermelon stalls, pineapple and oil palm plantations and jungle. As they approached the landslide area, the road surface changed from asphalt to gravel. In that area there were no oil companies opening up new roads. They stopped where the vehicular road ended, in the middle of a rubber plantation whose trees were currently in the last stages of losing their leaves, not far from Sei Kumbang and its river flowing towards Ogan. The sound of the river's little rapids was audible above the rustling of the *alang-alang* grass that was being buffeted about by the wind. The road siding had become a sort of terminal for heavy transport vehicles. Houses were scattered around it, set somewhat apart from each other, but all built to the same design. Rogam got out of the car and approached a group of people carrying rubber-tapping knives, and spoke to them in Komering, the local language. Then one of them began shouting as he ran towards a house nestling among a cluster of trees, from which a middle-aged woman appeared. Two young men in their twenties followed her. When they had emerged from the shadows of the trees, Wis could see that the face of one of the men was disfigured. The whole left side looked as if it had melted, leaving his skin and ear resembling those of a plastic doll that's caught fire then set again in an odd shape. His skin was rose-colored, without pores.

"*Mak*," Rogam greeted the woman. "We've got your daughter with us. She fell down a well and had to spend the night in the hospital."

Wis went to help the girl out of the car. But she screamed and kicked with her one good leg, knocking over a toolbox in the process. Wis couldn't understand what she was saying but it was quite clear that she didn't want to get out of the car. She crouched in the corner of the back seat, like a caged mouse deer, clutching her hands and knees to her chest so nobody could drag her out. Wis just stood there, helpless, but the two young men pushed their way into the car and hoisted her onto their shoulders like a suitcase, something they seemed accustomed to doing. When they put her down she remained in a squatting position, curled up like a porcupine under attack. Her mother tried to get her to stand up, but she just lay there cringing. Only her head stuck out, as she peered, with her terrified eyes, at the people standing around her. Wis had no idea of what was happening. Without thinking he went over to her, bent down and stretched out his hand to try and help her to get up. But she pushed him with such force that he toppled over backwards, and then she tried to make a run for it. Her injured leg put paid to that idea, and she fell flat on her face. The two young men dragged her along the path, ignoring her howls and moans. Bewildered, Rogam and Wis, who was still lying spread-eagled on the ground, watched the three figures as they disappeared down the path. Then they saw the girl being put into a sort of cage behind the house. Wis could hear her moaning pitifully when the two men had locked the door. The others watched in silence. A group of children momentarily looked up from their game – a competition involving rubber seeds – and laughed.

"Stop! Stop! What are you doing!" Wis rushed over to the two men who'd just taken the key from the lock.

"We have no choice. Our sister's mad. She's possessed by the devil."

"You can't lock her up like that..."

The cage, a meter and a half by two meters in size, was made of wood and bamboo. It stood there on short stumps like a little stage. It stank of urine and dampness. And there were flies everywhere. The girl squatted behind the bars sobbing, she wasn't howling any more.

"Let her go! She's just a child!" Wis shook one of the men by the shoulders.

But her mother came up to him. "Excuse me Mister," she said deferentially, as was the custom for a villager addressing a newcomer from the city, "It's not that we don't love her. It's just that we don't know what else to do." Her voice was weary and Wis turned to look at her. There was no sign of cruelty in the face of this forty-ish woman. She looked with empty eyes at her caged daughter.

The girl's name was Upi. The mother began to tell Wis about her lunatic daughter. When she was born, her head was so tiny that her father thought it was some sort of retribution for his having killed a turtle over by the lake in the early stages of his wife's pregnancy. And the child never learnt to speak, though her body developed as normal into that of an adolescent. Maybe because she could never master the language of humans, Satan took hold of her tongue. When she was in her teens she showed signs of being possessed and she became quite delinquent. It started when she developed the habit of rubbing her genitals up against the rubber trees as they were being tapped by the villagers, fortunately without taking her clothes off. Everyone would watch her – the boys with lust and the girls with embarrassment – but we just kept trying to care for her. But Satan too kept watch over her. As time went by she grew fond of animals as well, especially goats. And every time she would torture the animal, sometimes she would even kill it. Because she violated and tortured our neighbors' animals we had to restrain her. Initially we used wooden stocks on her ankles. But because that completely immobilised her and caused her a great deal of suffering we built this little hut and locked her inside. Apparently Satan likes menstrual blood. In the week before her unclean period she usually becomes very violent. Once her behavior normalizes, about a week after her period, we let her out of the cage. That's when she goes wandering off to the villages and other towns. We used to just let her go; we'd never had any reports of bad behavior. But once she went berserk for no apparent reason. Anson, her brother, found her in the kitchen, holding a duck between her legs and trying to strangle it. He yelled at her to stop and tried to rescue the duck. But Upi grabbed a bottle of the sulfuric acid that we use to dilute the rubber and poured it over him, maiming his face and blinding him in one eye. She's extremely dangerous. We're worried sick that she'll harm somebody else. So now we lock her up. A couple of days ago she managed to break off one of the bars that had gone a bit rusty.

Wis could hardly believe this, but he didn't give up. He said, "Can't you take her to a psychiatric hospital?"

But the mother sighed. "In Palembang? Where would I get the

money for that? As I told you, it's not that we're being deliberately cruel to her..."

Wis fell silent. He retreated into his own thoughts. He glanced at the girl in the cage but had to avert his eyes because he couldn't bear to see her suffering. But the overwhelming reality of his surroundings brought him back to earth. The village had a disjointed feel about it. There were about a hundred houses, all of them the standard three by six meters. But more than a third of them had been abandoned. *Alang-alang* grass had taken root inside the houses; it was visible through the windows and the empty doorways, whose wooden frames had succumbed to a combination of mold, termites and neglect. Vines hung down from the roofs like hair. And the rows of rubber trees that stretched as far as the eye could see looked like men in need of a shave and a good haircut, they were choked with weeds. A number of trees had toppled over, giving the area the appearance of a jungle rather than a plantation. The half-blind Anson explained that people were leaving because the price of rubber had fallen so drastically and the crop was continually infested by harmful fungi, the red fungi and the white fungi. It was no longer possible to earn a decent living from rubber farming. "My brother and I and our mother are still tapping rubber but our father and other brother have gone off to the city to work as laborers. There's no money to pay for treatment for Upi."

Wis looked again at the girl in the cage. She was powerless.

He was powerless to do anything about it.

That evening back in his bed at the parish, he tossed and turned like a fish being fried in a pan. He had witnessed suffering behind the façade of a modern city, but he had never before seen deprivation like what he had observed that afternoon. In Bantargebang people live among the rubbish of Jakarta's rich and greedy, and lunatics can wander through the neat manicured gardens of Taman Suropati.

But a mere seventy kilometers from the oil town of Perabumulih a girl is tortured, not as a result of greed but because the people are so far removed from modernity. And all I can do is lie here on this mattress?

When it was time for Upi's plaster cast to be removed, Wis requested five days leave, Monday afternoon until Saturday morning, from the head priest Father Westenberg. This time he took a chainsaw with him, along with a roll of fencing wire, a bag of cement and some zinc sheeting that he got from Kong Tek's hardware shop. The Chinese merchant gave it all to him for free. In addition he took food rations of instant noodles, a five kilogram sack of rice and preserved meat. Once again Rogam took him in Ichwan's company jeep. A young doctor from the local clinic accompanied them. At noon Rogam and the doctor headed back north but Wis stayed at Upi's village of Lubukrantau, one of the transmigration villages near Sei Kumbang. He had decided to ease Upi's suffering by building her a more pleasant and more sanitary cage, just as he had built a big cage for his father's turtledoves and bulbuls, because releasing them was tantamount to killing them. Bemused, Mak Argani, Upi's mother, and her two brothers let him go ahead. For the rest of the afternoon Wis pushed a wheelbarrow around the village collecting bits of concrete block that were lying on the ground around the abandoned houses, if nobody was watching he also pried stone off the walls of the houses, and wooden planks off the doors.

He succumbed to hunger quickly, his body unused to the physical labor. He boiled two packets of instant noodles and offered half to Upi. She was obviously interested in the food but didn't eat right away. She kept saying something over and over again, in a questioning tone. It wasn't until evening that he understood – when Upi's mother prepared a meal of boiled rice, taro leaves and a packet of the instant noodles he'd given her earlier in the day. One packet of instant noodles was the main course for all five of them. They didn't eat it as a carbohydrate-rich meal in itself. That evening he slept in Argani's house, which was basically just one room. There was one internal room, two meters by three, which served as the parents' bedroom. The brothers, Anson and Nasri, and Wis slept on the floor of the verandah, three meters wide by three meters long. The air was rife with the mingled smells of old cooking oil, acid and ammonia. But a thin strip of sky was visible through the window like a ray of hope. It looked like a blue sapphire against the blackness of the forest and the dimness of the walls. There was no electricity for tens of kilometers.

Early next morning, after a quick wash in the river, he set to work. The sun had reached the tops of the rubber trees because the southern hemisphere was approaching summer. The leaves were beginning to bud, a sign of recent regular rain, which usually began after three in the afternoon. For that reason Wis badly wanted Upi to get her new home before the rainy season began in earnest. Nasri helped him while Anson and Mak Argani were off tapping rubber. Wis showed him the plan he'd drawn on a piece of wax paper. The cage would consist of three main parts. A yard open to the sun and the rain, enclosed by a wire fence. A room with masonry walls, windows and good ventilation. And a separate toilet and bathroom. They began by digging a meter and a half deep trench for the toilet, hammering in the uprights and covering part of the surface with floorboards, and making a bamboo screen. That was all they managed to achieve before night fell. The next day Wis could barely move. Every one of his muscles was stiff and sore because, although he'd driven a tractor and cultivated plants at the agricultural institute, he'd never really done any hard labor. He hadn't brought any analgesics with him, certain as he was that he would be up to the task. He had been wrong; he was hurting all over. Wis worked with a perpetual grimace on his face as he tried to endure the pain while Upi observed him from her smelly cage. From time to time she would mutter something in her own language. These strange utterances would entice Wis to glance over at her. He would smile and talk to her about all manner of things. He kept encouraging Upi to talk, even though neither of them could understand the other's language. But in this way they managed to establish a communication of sorts. They could gauge each other's feelings through the tone and intonation of their voices. As time passed, each time they looked at each other Wis felt himself growing fond of her. He would look at her from time to time and realize with a start that compassion comes in unexpected guises after we've been immersed in sadness.

Upi's house wasn't finished by the fourth day, the day before Wis was supposed to be returning home. But he was reasonably satisfied – the walls were completed and the wire fence was in place. That evening, after he had put away his tools, he went over and looked into the girl's cage. Over the course of the previous four days, having spent so much time in each other's company, her suspicion had subsided. She got up and approached Wis, who was holding on to the bars.

"Look, Upi! Your golden cage will soon be finished. Next week I'll make you a sleeping platform and a dining table," he said proudly.

The girl responded with a smile and stroked Wis's knuckles as they clutched the bars. She touched the callouses that were beginning to form as a result of four days of manual labour. Wis said nothing because no woman had ever touched his fingers before, and he didn't quite know how to react. He felt he should take his hand away but he didn't want to hurt her feelings. Awkwardly he let her stroke him, and she stretched out her hand to touch his arm, grimy and sweaty as it was. Her lopsided gaze then shifted downwards, from his face to his stomach, coming to rest at his groin; her hand was on the bulge in his trousers before Wis realized what she was doing. He cried out in surprise and sprang backwards. He walked away and the girl cried out over and over again.

That night he could hear her moaning in her cage. The din made by the cicadas and the crickets wasn't enough to muffle the sound of her voice. He hadn't been asleep yet; he couldn't stop thinking about the girl, whose mental growth had been retarded despite her physical maturation. She was still young; she had a long life ahead of her. Wis had tried to build her a better prison, but what did the future hold for her out here in this desolate jungle of rubber trees? During his four days in the village Wis had made a note of the daily activities of the farmers. They had to go out and tap their trees every day so they could sell more resin and get a higher income. But because of this constant tapping the trees were aging quickly, like workers continually forced to work overtime. The trees had a very short lifespan and the rubber they produced was of a poor quality. The brokers and the rubber company then bought the low-grade rubber very cheaply; sometimes a kilo of latex didn't bring in enough to buy a kilo of rice. What would become of Upi if her family decided to pack up and leave? Would they build her a big cage in their new place? Where would they go? From her cage Wis could hear moaning and the rhythmic creaking of bamboo. He went to the back window and looked towards the cage. It was full moon and the sky was clear. He could see her in silhouette, rocking back and forth. Her bare feet poked through the bamboo bars of the cage, which glowed soft and golden against the blue background. Her legs and hips were wrapped around a large bamboo pole. Two minutes later she gave a cry and the hut stopped vibrating. Wis closed the window and lay down.

The following Monday Wis went back to Lubukrantau to finish Upi's house. For a moment she was dazzled by the light streaming into her new home, something she hadn't been used to in her dank old room. Then she prowled up and down like an animal in a wildlife park acclimatizing to its new cage. From the remains of her old cage Wis salvaged the biggest pole; it was about 1.8 meters high and twenty centimeters thick. He sanded it smooth and dragged it over to a shady spot, where he sat and pored over a photo from a magazine that he'd brought with him from Perabumulih. He shaped a small piece of wood into a triangle and attached it to the pole. He also carved a pair of eyes and a mouth around the triangle-nose, doing his best to copy the handsome wooden Sigalegale carving in the photo in front of him, the statue that adorned traditional Batak houses. He made a pair of arms as well, from sturdy branches, attaching them with sugar palm fiber, so they could move. Then he hoisted the makeshift statue onto his shoulder and carried it over to Upi's new house, where he secured it into place with cement solder.

"Upi! Come and meet your boyfriend! His name is Totem. Totem Phallus. You can masturbate with him. He's a good faithful man."

Upi looked briefly at the statue, muttered something, then looked back at Wis. He laughed brightly, proud of his work of art, and then seized Totem Phallus's hand and shook it. "This is *Abang*, Upi. Say hello to him!" he said. But the girl stood up and took hold of Wis by the wrist, no longer interested in the wooden man with the thin moustache. This unsettled Wis. She took his hand and placed it on her breast. He withdrew it quickly. No, Upi! You mustn't do that to me. Bewildered, he distanced himself from the cage and the girl, who was crying out for him. It was so hard for him to have to lock the door again, imprisoning the girl whose eyes never left his for a moment. Have I done the wrong thing? Did I offend her by making the statue? All I wanted to do was make your prison a bit more pleasant for you, Upi. I want you to have everything you need. Because I am powerless to liberate you.

He stopped at the back door of the house. He turned and saw that she had undone the buttons of her blouse. If I were a woman, or if you were a man, maybe it would be easier for us to be friends and I could ease your loneliness.

The more I am part of your suffering, the more I want to be with you. And Wis kept going back there. The more familiar he became with the plantation, the more worried he became about Upi's future. This concern was intensified one day when he arrived to find the village in uproar. Anson and two other young men were sitting on their sleeping platform, faces all bloodied. Some of the women were applying betel leaf compresses to their swollen faces. The villagers told him that there had been a raid. The guards had caught the three of them selling resin to the brokers. Their buckets had been confiscated and they were beaten up for stealing latex from the rubber company.

With a sense of foreboding, Wis sat down among them. He had already observed quite a lot. He knew that, under a government project called the "people's nucleus plantation" or PIR, these transmigrant farmers owed money to the rubber company for seeds, fertilizer, and the cost of clearing the land. Somewhere between five and nine million rupiah, to be paid off in installments over twenty-five years. So every time they sold latex to the company, thirty percent was deducted from their payment to pay off the debt. But recently the price of rubber had plummeted and sometimes they received less than five hundred rupiah per kilo of resin. So they had decided to sell to the brokers on the side; they usually paid more than the company, and the farmers could also buy rice and other necessities from them on credit. But now they were in trouble because the rubber company had sent out guards to patrol this remote plantation. Let's hope it was just a one-time thing, someone said.

When the crowd had begun to disperse, Wis went over to Upi's cage. It was a long time since he had been inside it. He would have liked to go in, but she obviously still had lustful designs on him. So he just stood outside and called out to her. She emerged from behind the dingy curtains that covered the doorway, smiling broadly. Wis gave her a box of biscuits. As usual they chatted, each in their own language. It depressed him to think that she was completely oblivious to the fact that her family was being dragged deeper and deeper into poverty. What can I do, Upi, to make sure that you don't end up in an even more vile place than this prison of yours?

As the clouds gathered on the tips of the woods, Wis helped Anson and Nasri to collect the resin cups. For the last three months he had been familiarizing himself with the ways of the rubber plantation. He felt as if he had become one of the trees, standing there in diagonal rows, the latex flowing behind their bark and oozing out of the gashes in their brown and white trunks. He often imagined himself as a rubber tree that had been cut, the cut oozing resin and the resin providing a livelihood for the people who collected it. Resin as redemption. At least for Upi.

The wet season had arrived like a great wave from the east, drenching the plantation. Through the water that fell in torrents outside the back door he could see Upi sheltered in her little room.

Father Westenberg called him the minute he got back to the parish house. His face was still grimy from the dust that had been churned up on the road on the journey home. It was a searingly hot day, but three previous days of continual rain had eroded the Baturaja-Tanjungagung road, and the wire embankments put in place by the Department of Public Works had been of little use. The vehicle he was travelling in, along with several others, had been held up for twenty-four hours. He knew that his boss would be annoyed with him for being so late and that he would have words with him about his frequent visits to Sei Kumbang.

They sat facing each other but the older man took charge of the conversation. A Dutchman with expertise in Malay languages, he spoke calmly about parochial matters. Wis listened attentively, aware that he was about to be reprimanded for neglecting his parish duties. At the very least, he would be censured for too often not being available when he was needed.

"I know you have plans for improving the lot of the farmers there. That's commendable. But serving and nurturing your congregation here is no less important," he said.

At first Wis said nothing. Then he apologized. "It's not my intention to trivialize the work of the church. It's just that I haven't been able to sleep since my first visit to the village." He wanted to add something about his feelings of guilt at sleeping on a comfortable mattress and eating the delicious food prepared and brought to him by the parish women, who had drawn up a cooking roster. He even felt guilty when all he could do was pray. He couldn't bear to stand by and watch these people go into decline, a decline which he believed could be halted with the implementation of a few of his ideas. Somewhat awkwardly, he asked for permission to do just that.

Father Westenberg folded his arms and gave a long sigh, as was his custom when he was deep in thought. Then he said: "You're young and you're enthusiastic. That's great. But we're part of an organization. Each of us, you and I, must surrender ourselves to it, so that the work is shared equally. What I'm saying is that we can't always do as we please. Decisions must be made in the appropriate manner within the system."

Wis sighed, because this meant that he would have to contact the Bishop for formal permission. The Bishop wasn't renowned for making decisions in a hurry. Especially concerning something that wasn't directly connected to Church business. And what was more, he would need Father Westenberg's recommendation. He looked at the old man, pleading with his eyes for his support in his approach to the Bishop, just as he had asked Romo Daru's help in ensuring that he get posted here.

After observing Wis for a while, compassion got the better of the Dutch priest and he acceded to Wis's request. What can I do for you? Without the blessing of the Bishop there's no money to carry out your plans. I imagine you don't have much money of your own. But the fact that you have chosen to be a diocesan priest will work in your favor, because it means you are allowed to manage a budget outside the direct control of the Order. If you can raise the money yourself I'm prepared to allow you to go there for three weeks each month. The fourth week must be spent here in the parish. If I can see any real results from your labors, I'm prepared to propose that the Bishop assign you categorical duties in the plantation.

Wis was so grateful he didn't know what to say. After he'd had a shower he sat down and wrote a letter to his father. This time it wasn't just to send news and his love, as usual, but also to ask for money, about five or six million rupiah, hardly a big amount for his father. For his part, he hated the thought of borrowing from the bank. Anyway, he rationalized to himself, he was an only child and his father, who hadn't remarried, would never have any grandchildren. There was no point in keeping the inheritance stashed away. The next day he also got in contact with Sarbini. This old friend of his father's was now a rubber broker in Sukasari, a Javanese transmigration area adjacent to Sei Kumbang, whose transmigrants were now considered local. Sarbini was a descendant of the Javanese laborers brought by the Dutch to the Deli region in the 1930s. He had done some military training but had then taken a job with the Bimas credit-plan scheme in the transmigration villages. Sarbini was thoroughly versed in the buying and selling network and with latex processing. Wis needed just those sorts of networks.

His father agreed to give him the money. Wis immediately

returned to Lubukrantau. Upi shrieked with delight when she heard his voice. But he only spent a few moments with her because he had important business to discuss with her mother and brothers.

As he poured ammonia into the storage tank, Wis proposed that he work with the Argani family on their two-hectare lot. He had been studying the plantation for four months now. Begun in 1976, the government PIR project hadn't been very successful. Apparently the initial clearing hadn't been thorough enough and the remaining stumps from the original forest still harbored a type of root mold. They called it white fungus. Now more than a quarter of the rubber trees had fallen down because they had been weakened by the fungus, like a leg ravaged by gangrene. The impoverished farmers planted yams among the rows of rubber trees to supplement their diet when they couldn't afford rice, but the tubers only served to spread the fungus even further. The company itself had no money to fix the problem, especially since the farmers were always late with their debt repayments. And Sei Kumbang was so remote that more often than not the fertilizer and plant sprays simply didn't arrive. The long distance and the corrugated roads between the village and the cooperative, combined with the effect of the smokehouses, meant that the latex would often undergo a chemical reaction from being shaken around and exposed to high temperatures before it even reached the buyers. This was why Wis's plans included building a modest processing plant in the village and improving the quality of the crop.

The family trusted Wis completely, even though they couldn't understand his concern for Upi. After Argani and her two sons had agreed to Wis's proposal they watched curiously as he went over to her cage. "How are you, Upi? I'm going to be spending a bit more time here with your brothers. Are you happy about that? Pray that your plantation will become fertile again and you can get a nicer house."

Wis and the two brothers began by saving the trees that were still healthy. Next they cleaned the roots that were just starting to be attacked by the clinging hypha threads. After that they destroyed the trees that were beyond saving. This was no mean feat. They had to chop down about a hundred trees, digging out their roots so that not a trace remained in the soil, then they had to burn them in order to destroy the pernicious fungus. *Rigidoporus lignosus*. Its young cobs were orange. But Wis couldn't confine himself to working on the Argani family's crop. They had to improve the neighbors' crops as well because the smokehouse he had planned would be inefficient if there was only a small supply of latex. So he covered long distances on foot as he checked the trees for disease, including the trees that had been abandoned. He went as far as a plantation that bordered on virgin forest. There were signs that the wild boars frequented the area. He came across an old bamboo trap, a bit like Upi's old cage, that was now matted with vines.

Suddenly he felt intensely weary. He sat down and leaned against a fallen tree and took his water bottle from his rucksack – his hand was shaking. But the bottle was empty. He laid his head back for a moment, listening for the sound of a nearby spring. When he heard spattering noises coming from somewhere he got to his feet, legs trembling. His blood stayed in the lower part of his body, it didn't flow to his head where he needed it, and so his vision was blurred. He saw stars in front of him, as if his optical nerves couldn't function properly without their supply of blood. He steadied himself by holding on to a branch of the tree. But when the purplish stars subsided he saw a cobra right there next to his foot. Its triangle-shaped head was erect and its neck was puffed up. Both its copper-colored eyes were focussed on Wis's knee.

He was terrified; he had never been at such close quarters with an agitated snake. And he didn't want to die at this early stage of his project. Showing its fangs, the cobra was clearly ready to attack. At the very moment when Wis realized that the snake was not going to show him any mercy, he heard the voices again. The familiar voices, the voices he hadn't heard for so long, the voices that always used to come from behind. They were faint at first then gradually became louder, though Wis couldn't make out what they were saying. But he saw the cobra's neck deflate and its head stop moving. Then it slid off.

He was dizzy from fear. Little blue dots, ant-like, appeared before his eyes again. Before his vision failed completely he saw three figures standing in a circle around him. But a few moments later everything went black. He collapsed.

It was four days before he regained consciousness. His arms were a mass of intravenous tubes, providing liquids and nourishment to his exhausted, emaciated body. He was ashamed at his lack of stamina. The nurse told him that he was suffering from severe dehydration and malnutrition. Too much work and not enough nourishment. "You were lost in the jungle for two days," the sister said. "People were out looking for you but they couldn't find you. Did you lose your way? It was lucky that you managed to find your way home before collapsing near the house. The tigers are almost extinct but that doesn't mean there aren't still some around. The girl in the cage made a great hullabaloo to let her brothers know you were sprawled there in the back yard. Then they brought you here yesterday afternoon."

Wis retreated into his own thoughts. Once again he kept the mystery to himself. Because he was convinced that he'd found what he'd lost in the past. The thing that had driven him to come back to this area. But now he'd also discovered something that called to him even more strongly: the rubber trees, and Upi.

1990. SOMETHING HAPPENED TO UPI.

By then the farmers in Lubukrantau had begun tapping the young rubber trees they'd planted six years earlier, replacing those that had been attacked by fungus. Wis had bought some of the seeds from the cooperatives and cultivated them himself. Before the trees had matured, the farmers had kept on with tapping the old ones and had planted vegetables that were suitable for intercropping such as soybeans. Then, with the assistance of Sarbini, they managed to find a market for the bundles of smoked sheets that they produced in their modest smokehouse. At night, as he gazed at the stars touching the perimeters of the rubber plantation and the trees where the birds rested for the night, Wis would silently pray to God to continue to protect the plantation. He would listen for a while to the night sounds of the forest. Then he would look in on Upi who was much happier here than she would be in a psychiatric hospital.

The Bishop had granted his request to work in the plantation. But one week in each month he returned to Perabumulih to help Father Westenberg, to whom he felt he owed a debt of gratitude. On one occasion he stayed for a fortnight because the old man was ill with a fever. Upon his return to Lubukrantau Mrs. Argani greeted him with some shocking news. Two men had broken into Upi's little house and raped her, leaving bite marks on her chest. Upi was now twenty-one.

Wis swallowed and bit his lip so hard it almost bled. "How is she?" he asked, rushing to her house before her mother had even finished telling him the story. He felt powerless to do anything, especially since she may well have enjoyed the experience. He had never known what to do about her sexual urges.

"Upi's okay," replied Anson, falling into step beside him. And when he got to the cage there she was, laughing with delight at seeing him again.

"What if she's pregnant?" Wis said sharply to Anson.

"I don't know. If she has a baby my wife will look after it. But Upi's never gotten pregnant before." Anson had been married for three years. He was always curious about why Wis, seven years his senior, had never married, and Wis had never felt inclined to explain. Anson glanced at his sister for a moment then looked at Wis as if he had something to tell him. "There's something more serious," he said.

Wis turned around, a frown deeply etched in his forehead. Tensely he listened to what the man had to say. Anson was convinced that the rape was part of a campaign of terror by a mob who wanted to take over their land. They did it deliberately in order to intimidate us into handing over the plantation. Then he took Wis to the dam to look at the windmill that they'd built as a mini electricity generator for their smokehouse. In the last three years it had produced five thousand watts of power, enough to enable the village (which now consisted of about eighty houses and a prayer house) to be brightened by electric lights and radios. The electricity itself was a source of wonder for the villagers. But now the windmill had been toppled over.

Wis stared at the destruction in front of him, incredulous that anyone could do such a thing. "Let me check out the damage. You go home!" he said to Anson, his voice trembling. "Go home! Sort out that fertilizer I brought with me. There's urea and KC1." When Anson didn't move immediately, Wis became very abrupt. He wanted to be alone. The moment Anson had gone, he went inside the windmill, into which he had invested so much time and energy. The turbine had been smashed; it looked as if someone had taken to it with an axe. In order to repair it he would have to buy a new generator. He took a deep breath and pressed his forehead against the damp wall. Something seemed to be caught in the base of his throat. He let a tear or two fall, then gave way to his grief, weeping silently.

He recalled a visit by some men the previous year. Their faces flashed into his mind, the faces of wild boars: greedy, cruel, spiky-haired. There had been four of them, dressed in safari suits, and they had come into the smokehouse when he and Anson were sorting out sheets of rubber.

"Who are you?" Wis asked.

"Officials."

"From where?"

"Just officials. It doesn't matter where from," one of them replied.

"What do you want?"

"We need to see a Mr..." he looked at his notes for a moment, "Argani."

"That's me. Anson bin Argani." Anson stepped forward without taking the cigarette out of his mouth. His scarred face gave him a swaggering sort of appearance, especially since he'd recently taken to covering his blind left eye with a black patch. The men stepped back a little.

They only spoke briefly. "We're here to carry out instructions from the Governor." One of them held up a piece of paper with government letterhead on it, but he didn't give it to Anson. "According to the Governor's decree of 1989, the Sei Kumbang transmigration area is to be turned into a palm oil plantation. The successful tendering company has been appointed, it's Anugrah Lahan Makmur." He paused for a moment, looked around the processing plant, glanced out the window, and turned to Anson again. "We notice that this village is the only one that hasn't yet signed the agreement with the company."

Wis interrupted, "You should know that we have never agreed to replace our rubber trees with oil palms. And this plantation is not the property of the company."

But the man replied more vehemently, "Our business is with Mr. Argani. Not with you!"

Anson immediately chimed in, repeating what Wis had said in an equally irate manner. "We had heard that the company was losing money here and that they had handed over the plantation to a new company that wanted to turn it into an palm oil plantation. But not all the rubber crops in Sei Kumbang have been a failure. Ours has been profitable and we have always paid off our installments on time. We've already started tapping the new trees that we planted. This village is prospering. If the company wants to turn the failed rubber plantations into palm oil plantations, let them. But don't let them touch our trees. The farmers are the ones who are supposed to benefit from transmigration, aren't they?"

"You can raise all those matters with the company officials. We're just here to convey the orders of the Governor."

Then the four men left, leaving an ultimatum: the people of Lubukrantau must sign the agreement and cut down their rubber trees. The company would distribute the palm oil seeds and the villagers would have to plant them. If they hadn't complied within a month the bulldozers would be sent in to raze the trees. There would be no other way, they stressed. Then they drove off in their jeep that had a company logo, the letters ALM and a silhouette of an oil palm with an orange sun, on the driver's door and the hood.

When the sound of the jeep's engine had died down, Wis sent some of the workers off to see what they could find out from the neighboring villages. They returned with the news that the household heads in the surrounding villages had indeed signed a piece of paper. And what was on it? asked Wis. It was a blank sheet of paper, they answered. How could anyone put their signature on a blank sheet of paper? Because they would be given a share of the palm oil seeds. Anyway, the officials said it was more practical this way; it was a nuisance for the company if it had to provide all the details of the agreement. Not everybody could read in any case. What was the point of giving a written contract to someone who was illiterate? Wis was stunned. What if their signatures were appended to a statement transferring all the farmers' land to the company, or to these officials?

"I don't trust them, Anson," said Wis. "How difficult can it be for a company to make a copy of the contract for each person?" Then he asked Anson to organize a village meeting. Since they'd built the smokehouse on the Argani family's land, which was managed by Anson, people had begun to regard Anson as one of village elders of Lubukrantau. At the meeting in the smokehouse Wis warned the villagers never to sign a blank piece of paper. If we have to sign an agreement, we must know first what it entails.

Three weeks later, when the four men came back in their company jeep, an altercation broke out. They ordered the entire village to assemble. Wis, Anson and three other men, middle-aged elders, insisted that the village had appointed them as spokesmen for the discussions. But one of the men approached Wis and barked at him, "We've investigated this village. You're not a resident! Where's your ID card?"

"He's my brother!" said Anson, covering Wis's confusion. The three others also came to his defense.

Grumbling, the four men explained the terms of the agreement: the villagers were to plant and cultivate the seeds provided to them by the company, with a salary of one thousand six hundred rupiah a day, and a share of the harvest. But Wis, Anson and the others insisted on a condition: We'll only discuss this matter with the villagers when the company has issued a copy of the agreement to every household head. We also want to do our negotiations directly with the company. Because he suspected that these officials were out for all the profit they could get. Irate, the four men left. Wis thought he saw them talking in the car, pointing at him. Not long after this incident he heard that various people in surrounding villages had been accusing him of trying to convert the Lubukrantau villagers to Christianity and of teaching the Argani family to hunt and eat wild boar.

Because he felt that there would not be a quick resolution to the matter, Wis went to Palembang, Lampung and Jakarta, taking with him photographs of the village and a detailed report about the progress being made there. He visited newspaper offices and non-government organizations. He talked passionately and at length with everyone he met and gave them the report. He urged them: if you possibly can, come and see our village for yourself. Once the newspapers had begun publishing articles and sending their journalists to the remote spot, the four men stopped bothering them with their blank pieces of paper. Their attempt to decimate the village was postponed for months, for almost a year.

But now Wis understood what they were up to. They were using different tactics. Lubukrantau was surrounded by villages that had agreed to convert to oil palm. Bulldozers had already begun to knock down the rubber trees. The acrid smell of smoke hung in the air as the workers burnt the tree stumps. They were being squeezed out. Terror had begun to descend on the village. It had started with the occasional early-morning discovery of a young rubber tree that had been felled, as if it had been knocked over by a wild boar. Then their animals began to disappear, one by one. The road was obstructed by roadblocks. Now the windmill had been destroyed and Upi had been raped. How much longer can we hold out?

Wis realized that his tears had left two wet circles on the chest of his shirt. He was worried sick about the fate of the village and the fate of Upi. He was like a desert town under siege, his well controlled by the enemy. God, have you allowed this to happen? Then he wiped his face and returned to the house. Darkness was falling and there was no electricity. But Anson had gathered the adult villagers together in the smokehouse, instructing a number of young men to stand guard outside. He went to find Wis and asked him to join in.

They sat cross legged in a circle around two humming kerosene lamps, about sixty men and ten elderly women, the acrid smell of rubber heavy in the air. Their tapping knives still hung from their waists. The younger women remained in their houses with the children. Exhausted, Wis sat down in a corner; he could no longer think straight. His head was bowed, his arms rested on his knees and he massaged his brow. He lit a cigarette. But Anson asked him to open the emergency meeting.

Wis refused. "You do it! I've only just got here; I don't know what's been happening." When he saw everyone's hopeful eyes turned in his direction he attempted to revive his sagging spirits a little. In the yellowish light their eyes were deep black. The further they were from the lamp the darker their eyes seemed to be.

Then he heard Anson talking. He watched the young man, several years his junior, fervidly explaining that the palm oil company that had taken over the rubber company was owned by a Chinese businessman. "The Chinese are colonizing us. The Indonesians are being turned into little more than poor laborers." And Wis realized that their bitterness had been transformed first into profound anger and then into a deep and troubling suspicion. He thought about Kong Tek, who had been so generous with his provision of building materials. He thought about the Chinese journalists who had visited the village. He thought also about how the Chinese always had to pay more for their passports and ID cards. And here was Anson, talking about the issue so simplistically. Wis felt he must interrupt. "Please, Anson!" He held up his hand. "I just want to remind you that we got all the materials for building the smokehouse we're sitting in very cheaply from a Chinese trader in Perabumulih. Some of it was free. Secondly, the shares of Anugrah Lahan Makmur aren't owned solely by that one Chinese businessman; he's in partnership with a Javanese man and a big Batak plantation-owner. Thirdly, the bosses of the palm oil company have been paying native-born Indonesians – dark skinned people just like us – to intimidate us. To destroy, to steal, to rape. They're native mongrels! Bastards from around here!" He stopped for a moment when he realized he was letting anger get the better of him.

He watched the reaction of the villagers. They were still listening to him, some of them with bewildered expressions on their faces. He continued calmly, "The way I see it our problem is not dealing with the Chinese issue. But rather with what we are going to do with our plantation."

A general hubbub erupted in the shed, with varying degrees of intensity, until Anson put an end to it with his unambiguous declaration: we have to defend our rubber plantation! The room echoed with the thunderous agreement of those present. Wis observed their faces and it occurred to him that the rubber plantation they had been working on together had gradually come to represent the only thing that was real to these people. He thought about his chance meeting with Upi – six years previously – that had resulted in his close involvement with the plantation. But would they now be able to defend their trees from that bigger, stronger power? Should they hold out? And prolong this campaign of terror? Isn't our ultimate goal a prosperous village? Wouldn't it be best for them just to agree to replace the rubber trees with oil palms, as long as the contract is beneficial to them? Oil palms can also be harvested after five years.

When Wis posed these questions the shed once again resounded with the din of their vigorous debate. He saw that their anger was directed at some intangible threat. "This is a matter of honor. They're no better than the Dutch. They just tell us to plant whatever suits their needs. We have to stand up for our rights!" This passionate plea came from Seruk, a young man who wasn't even old enough to shave. Wis looked at him in astonishment. Until now he'd only known him as a docile boy who worked in the mill. Where had he learned to speak like that? In silence Wis listened as they argued and debated in an attempt to reach a resolution. Although he'd been living with these people for six years, he had had no idea of what they were thinking.

His contemplation was interrupted when Mrs. Argani suddenly called out, "What do you think, *Bapak* Wis? Should we resist or negotiate?" Even though he'd been living in her house all this time, in front of other women she always addressed him as *Bapak*, the polite form of address.

"What do you think, brother?" Anson repeated his mother's question when Wis didn't respond straight away.

For once Wis didn't want to be the one to make the decision on behalf of the plantation. How things had changed. He used to be so strident, so confident; he had the ability to inspire hope when everything seemed hopeless, his energy levels never flagged. But now he had grave doubts about the consequences, of what might happen to these people. It saddened him greatly because for the first time he felt that he was not truly part of their community. After all I don't stand to lose a thing if the plantation is destroyed. I can go back to the church where the parish ladies wait on me hand and foot, where I preach to them and give them the sacrament. Or I can lead retreats in Catholic schools in the city, where the girls all fall in love with me and send me letters and poems. But for the farmers this plantation is their life. Whatever I do I'll never really endure the suffering that they experience. Wis was very reluctant to make a decision on something he didn't have a stake in. But they were waiting for his answer. He just looked up and said, very wearily: "You draw up a proposal! I'll support whatever decision you come to." Because I have no stake in this gamble.

Then he counted the people present. There were about seventy.

This meant that the whole population of the village was between one hundred and fifty and two hundred. *What can I do for them? Maybe I could dismantle the smokehouse and rebuild it somewhere else? In nearby Sukasari, for example, eliciting the help of Sarbini?*

As he sat there thinking he suddenly heard voices coming from behind him. This time they weren't muffled, they were loud and clear, shouting directly into his ear. They seemed to be telling him something without actually saying anything. He leapt to his feet and rushed outside, yelling, "Anson! Your wife! Your wife!"

It was only about seventy meters from the smokehouse to Anson's house but another shed blocked it from view, so the young men on guard outside couldn't actually see it. But Wis ran to the house, certain that something was wrong. Anson blindly followed him. The rest of the crowd dispersed and headed in the same direction. Some of them got to the house first. The others brought up the rear with torches. When the first group of men got to the house they saw a shadow flash past and disappear into the trees. A number of people gave chase, although without electricity the night was very dark. Anson pushed his way into the house and found his wife naked and the trousers of a security guard discarded on the floor. She was sobbing and coughing violently, as if she'd just been choked. "There were two of them," she managed to gasp. From the kitchen came the sound of a tin can falling on the floor. The second man, who had been hiding, tried to escape, but the villagers had surrounded the house. In a matter of seconds they had caught the semi-naked man and dragged him to the smokehouse. Sickened, Wis saw Anson wipe semen from his wife's thigh.

Turmoil had descended upon the village. The women and children were herded into the prayer house. Mrs. Argani and a number of the other women tended to Arson's wife there and the others did a roll call of the village girls. Wis checked on Upi and asked one of the village boys to guard her cage, and then he went back to the smokehouse. As he reached the doorstep he saw the formless body of the man. His blue shirt was darkened by blood. His legs were bent at an odd angle as if they'd been dislocated, with the sole of his feet pointing in opposite directions. A thick dark color covered his groin. Wis couldn't see his face because people were still circling around, kicking him. In their hands he saw rubber-tapping knives dripping red. The man was obviously dead.

"We haven't got the other one yet!" yelled a man who'd just come in from the forest.

"Let's go after him. He'll be headed towards his guard post."

"Just set fire to the post!"

The crowd moved to a different location, like ants moving from one pile of sugar to another. Anson was so enraged that he decided to lead a mob of villagers in an attack on the police guard post. Wis was a bundle of indecision. He wanted to stop Anson but his resoluteness suddenly deserted him. He had lost all confidence in himself. Because he wasn't one of them. *Their cross is not my cross.* He wasn't a woman so he had no comprehension of the humiliation of rape, and he didn't have a wife so he couldn't fully empathize with Anson's fury. Suddenly he felt utterly insubstantial. Suddenly he felt he had no voice.

"Anson!" he cried with the only sound left in his throat. "Leave a few people behind to watch over the village."

As the mob of men disappeared into the shadows of the forest, Wis remained rooted to the step of the prayer house, watching the women inside lying on the green mats with their small children in their arms. It was only then that he realized that he'd been left with only seven or eight young boys to guard these women and children. He felt lonely and afraid as he sensed their eyes upon him, the only adult male remaining in the village, the man they had been relying on all this time to help them tend their plantation. *But have I got* what it takes to protect them in a situation such as this? What does it mean to be a man?

"Is everyone here?" he asked the women, trying to take charge of his emotions.

They replied in the affirmative. Wis then asked the women to pray. "Pray with all your heart, as passionately as you can. God willing, our prayers will dissipate everyone's anger." May God pacify the hearts of the men who may be about to besiege us.

Then he turned and left, surveying the area in front of the prayer house. He told one of the boys to cover the dead man's body with a sarong and to clean up the spilled blood. The others he dispatched in pairs to keep watch. When they'd gone he peered in the direction that Anson and his mob had gone, as if he was anxious that they might soon return. The melodious hum of the women praying quelled his anxiety but he felt that God was abandoning the village.

It was past midnight and none of the men had returned. Wis was getting more worried by the minute. He'd been keeping track of the boys on patrol by making a mental note of each time they passed by. Then the thought occurred to him that he should bring Upi over to join the women in the prayer house. It wasn't right to leave her alone in these circumstances. He went into the prayer house to see if Mrs. Argani would be able to look after her.

At the very moment that he opened his mouth to speak he heard the squeal of brakes. It had to be a jeep of some sort by the number of doors that were slammed. There was the approaching sound of several pairs of heavy footsteps. Wis felt his blood freeze momentarily, because he knew it wasn't Anson.

"Keep praying," he said hoarsely. And he didn't get the chance to ask about Upi. Then he went outside and encountered five burly men lined up in front of the building. They were identically dressed in black bandannas, tight black T shirts, black cargo pants and black boots. All five of them stood with legs astride and fists clenched. Wis made eye contact with them, and each party waited for the other to speak.

"What do you want?" he began eventually, after taking due account of their intimidating body language and their ice-cold eyes. All five remained motionless, like a row of heroes of the Revolution. But from the direction of the houses he could hear the harsh shrill shouts of someone issuing commands: "Come on out! Everybody out!" Wis estimated that there must be ten more of them out there breaking doors down. Where were the young boys on patrol?

Glancing at the road for a moment he noticed three jeeps and a dual-cab pickup truck parked in the siding. One of the men made a move as if he intended to force his way into the prayer house. Wis tried to stop him, "Please don't bother the women and children!"

"We are under instructions not to hurt the women and children," replied the man as he approached the step.

"This is a prayer house. Kindly remove your shoes if you want to go in!"

The sound of the women praying was reaching a crescendo.

"I just want to check it out." The man's boots, which were laced right to the knee, remained firmly on his feet. He just peered into the room, as if he was doing a head count, then turned and said, "So everyone's here?"

Wis said nothing but the man read the "yes" in his eyes. He nodded to his four mates. And there was the sound of orders being barked out. A minute later Wis saw smoke rising from the smokehouse, then from the Argani family's house and then from the other houses. He screamed as he remembered Upi, whom he hadn't been able to bring to her mother. He rushed to rescue her. But two of the black-uniformed thugs caught him and pinned his arms back, pushed him in the back until his chest and the side of his face touched the ground and handcuffed him, all before the scream had left his throat. They were quick and well-practiced. He had time to catch sight of the three others guarding the door of the prayer house, preventing the women from coming out, before someone blindfolded him and crammed a clump of cloth into his mouth. He was aware of several men hauling him and throwing him into a car that quickly fired up and sped off. He could smell fire and burning rubber. And the sound of the women praying, fading rapidly into the distance, until finally it was gone.

He struggled and writhed and tried to call out to them as the car sped along, to tell them that there was still a girl in the burning village. Finally someone took the blindfold off and asked angrily, "What do you want!" But they hadn't taken the cloth out of his mouth. The car stopped and the two men who'd been sitting either side of him got out. Then Wis felt something crushing his skull.

He felt as if he'd died. And he was distraught because God obviously didn't exist. Christ had clearly not saved him, because he was here in the valley of death, a long silent oppressive corridor, and he was falling, falling at terrifying speed into a bottomless well. Every bone in his body hurt. He could hardly move his hands even though they were no longer handcuffed; they'd been forced into such an awkward position for so long. When his eyes became accustomed to the light he saw that he was in a room about four meters by four meters. There was a door and two high air vents, but it was dark outside. The color of night. And he was wearing nothing but a pair of underpants which he didn't even think was his. When he checked he saw that they were a pair of light blue women's pants, edged with lace. So he knew that he had been the object of torture and ridicule by these people. There was a piece of bread and a glass of water by his side. He consumed them both because he was very hungry. He knew that he would be here for the long haul and that nobody would be able to help him because this was an illegal kidnapping. None of the newspapers would find out about this because he was the only Lubukrantau villager who had any contact with the outside world. The church might look for him but they wouldn't know where to start. Father Westenberg had no access to the villagers. Wis himself had no idea who had kidnapped him and where he was being imprisoned. This obviously wasn't a real jail. Then he remembered Upi and began to weep. This time he allowed himself to succumb to his tears.

At that point the death of the girl seemed to change everything: he was no longer afraid about what might happen to him, because he felt there was nothing left that was worth defending.

Nevertheless the torture to which he was subsequently subjected caused his body to tremble. He felt a shiver of fear each time he was led to the interrogation room and told to sit down, or was left standing, while he tried to guess what sort of tactics they would use this time. He could never see for himself because he was always blindfolded. Sometimes they put lit cigarettes to his skin, sometimes they put his fingers in a clamp, sometimes they whipped him, sometimes they put an electrical charge through his neck, sometimes they just kicked and punched him. No one tactic was preferable to the others. He had never before endured such pain.

Wis didn't know whether they were torturing him to exact some sort of revenge or because they really didn't believe his confession. It was obvious that none of them could fathom that his involvement with Lubukrantau had developed out of his compassion for the crazy, crippled Upi, upon whom he had never laid a finger. That's bullshit, they said. You were trying to establish some sort of power base among the farmers! You were trying to overthrow a legally elected government! And they kept up their torture so he would confess, even though he had nothing more to confess. When his hands and feet were being squeezed in a clamp, even Wis sometimes began to ask himself whether Upi was truly the motivation behind his work in the plantation, and on those occasions he simply agreed with their accusations. Eventually the excruciating pain forced out a story that had never even occurred to him before, a story which satisfied his torturers: He was actually a Communist disguised as a priest. He had studied liberation theology in South America, in some petty banana republic or was it a pineapple republic, and now he had come back to Indonesia to spread the doctrine. He was setting up a mass movement among the peasants with the aim of starting a revolution to establish the socialist state of Sumatra. Because the time was nigh for the kingdom of God. And this corrupt republic must be sent to a fiery grave forthwith. In an inaccessible area of protected forest on the Pasemah plateau, behind the coffee plantations that were now fragrant with the smell of seeds recently excreted by the civet cats, he'd set up a market garden. He'd built a fortress around it and assembled an armory of weapons, with the help of the peasants and the local Kubu people. The Lubu people too. They had already been converted to Christianity; the next step was to convert them to Communism. There were about a thousand of them in all. They had a utopian dream of creating their very own Eden here on earth, and they planned to replace the president and, most importantly, the territorial military commands.

As time went by he began to derive a perverse sort of pleasure from his own lies. Because this was the only way he could laugh at himself and at the stupidity and insanity of these people. It afforded him a form of escape. Every time the opportunity presented itself he would turn the pain into humor. Like the time they moved the electrical nodes from behind his ears to his penis. After he had recovered from the shock of being thrown backwards by the impact, he managed to raise a laugh. It won't bother me if you chop a bit off it. Because I only use it to piss. It doesn't need much length for that. But don't cut off my little finger, because I need that to pick my nose. His torturers assumed that the pain was sending him mad.

He was naked. His penis and his wounds were exposed to the world.

He awoke and felt that he was the size of a head. Just a head. No body. He didn't exist outside his own head. He had no fingers, no heart. It was dark. Is it because it's night or am I in the womb? Because it was warm and watery. Then there was the flash of a falling star. That was the first thing he saw. But the flash wasn't an asteroid or a meteor; it was the fetal membranes that had broken. He was being sucked into a vortex, into a keloid bubble. Then, when the membranes had been completely torn away, the first thing he saw was the face of his mother above a pair of mountainous breasts. There was snow on her nipples. Drops of milk. It seemed that Mother had just had a baby. The beads of sweat and the pain had been transformed into joy. The second thing he saw was stands of bamboo and trees, which became darker and darker as they stretched into the distance, and which were the dwelling places of thousands of snakes, of hundreds of ferocious species, and of evil spirits and fairies. *Lela lela ledhong – yen ing tawang ana lintang, when there are stars in the sky.* Then he saw another sign up there in the clouds, look it's a red dragon with seven heads and ten horns and its tail is sweeping the stars down to earth. They call him Satan, the old snake. And this creature snatched the new-born baby and took it into the forest and the woman ran to the desert where God had prepared a place where she could shelter for one thousand two hundred and sixty days. Wis hit his mother, over and over again, for letting it happen. Because his little sister was still alive even though she was dead, but why did they put her in a coffin. Because he sensed something else, something close to Mother that Father didn't know about, something very close, there was love there. There was a dream, there were torturers. Soldiers, nails, electric shock cables.

There was one thing that made Wis yearn for the interrogation sessions. Through the questions they asked he tried to gauge what was happening outside, what had happened to the village, to Anson and the others. He managed to piece together the facts that Anson and his mob had set fire to the security guard's post and the divisional police headquarters, and that they'd killed one official before fleeing. Apparently they'd not been captured yet; why else would these people be pressing Wis to disclose the location of their hideout. The village had been sealed off, nobody was allowed in, and the women and children had been moved to a refugee camp. No doubt some of them had been interrogated about his activities. So Upi must be dead. He couldn't find out for sure because they were only interested in asking about things that they considered relevant and important. Besides, his mouth hurt so much that before he could manage to articulate his questions clearly, they lost patience with him.

He felt a sense of relief when they tortured him into disclosing Anson's whereabouts, because it meant that he hadn't been caught. And when he returned to his cell he would pin his hopes on Anson remaining at large. But he could no longer put his hopes into prayer. After all the hardships they had gone through God had not saved them. Either He didn't want to or He wasn't able to. Or He didn't in fact exist. Wis felt unspeakably lonely.

Then for three days they didn't use the electricity on him. They just kicked and punched him like a ball and occasionally they would burn him with a cigarette butt. At moments when there was a respite from pain he began to feel uneasy about this change of tactic. What if the electrical cables were being used to torture Anson, whom they may have captured. At that moment he realized that there was something even more painful than being tortured, and that was watching your friends being tortured. He was terrified that they might bring Anson into the room and pulverize him before his very eyes. His sense of humor began to elude him. But he was relieved when they started to interrogate him about some organization in Lampung that had assembled an armory of weapons. This obviously had nothing to do with Anson. And he overheard someone mention that the torture equipment was being used on this other group.

Wis counted the days by observing the sliver of light that came through the air vents high up near the ceiling. It was the only way he could tell if it was day or night. If he'd been counting correctly, he'd been here for fourteen days. When would they get tired of torturing him, especially now his stories were starting to dry up? What would happen to him when they got bored and had run out of questions? The day before he had heard one of the torturers, a man who seemed a bit more intelligent than the others, tell the others that Wis's confession was just bullshit. And he was right! This guy, new on the scene, seemed to have a bit more common sense than the others. That day he hadn't yet been taken out of his cell, although he felt as if it must be getting late in the day. He began to wonder if his torture had come to an end with the arrival of this new guy. A feeling of desolation suddenly came over him. The interrogations, despite the extraordinary pain they inflicted on him, afforded him some contact with other people and gave him the chance to find things out. They enabled him to laugh at their stupidity and his own.

Here in the cell there was just his bruised body and swarms of mosquitoes. He had time to dwell on the minor ailments he was suffering, a cold and dizzy spells. He began to miss human contact. He missed everybody. His mother and his father. What would Father do if he knew what was happening to me? He'd probably be even more hurt and humiliated than I am myself. Hopefully he won't hear about it. He missed Father Westenberg, Mrs. Argani, the fiery Anson, Upi. The smell of the rubber plantation after the rain. The sound of people working in the smokehouse. He could no longer even cry.

But he missed the others. Where had the voices gone? The voices that have always made me know I was alive, the voices that brought me back here? It's true that they always come out of the blue, at times when I'm least expecting them. Wis wanted more than anything for them to be with him right now. Please come, please, come to me! But the day went by and the voices did not respond to his plea. The only voice he heard was that of the man who brought his food, and Wis would have liked so much to have had a chat with him.

At night the air was always thick with mosquitoes. For two days he hadn't slept, in the hope that they would take him out to talk, even though it would also mean being beaten up. Now he was feeling very fatigued and weary. He didn't even notice the mosquitoes. But he was having trouble breathing. His eyes were accustomed to the dark and he could see blackish smoke seeping through the bars of his cell. It was gradually becoming thicker. He could smell carbon dioxide. In his semi-conscious state it occurred to him that the place was on fire. He became alert for a moment but he was overcome by lethargy and nausea. And he said to himself: Okay, this is it. I just want to go to sleep. Maybe forever. He could see the flames beginning to lick at the door frame. He knew that he was being poisoned. He would die before the fire even got to him.

But he heard the voices. It was true, the voices that he'd been longing to hear, the voices that had deserted him while he'd been in prison. They were buzzing around his head like mosquitoes, as if trying to wake him up or to befuddle him. Then he felt the energy seeping into his body, life was being poured into his bones. And he felt weightless, like he imagined a body must feel when it was passing from one life to the next; his emaciated body suddenly seemed to have an excess of energy. He felt as if he could fly. He got up and pushed down the door that was already alight and ran through the burning corridor. He ran, he ran, he floated, some invisible force directing his steps. And he reached the last door, the one that took him outside. He was in a field planted with oil palms. There were stars and fresh air. He kept running until he heard someone yell, "My God! Wis! It's Wis!"

It was Anson's voice. *"Allahu Akbar."*

Wis felt someone catch him as he fell. He saw the faces of Anson and some of the other young men from Lubukrantau. Then he succumbed to exhaustion. The powers seemed to have deserted him. They flew off into the distance.

Hastily they left, disappearing into a row of young oil palms whose lower branches were still touching the ground. Behind them they could hear the crackling of wooden palings as they went up in flames, and the explosion of gas cylinders.

The young men took turns carrying Wis. On the way Anson told him that he had planned to set fire to this new oil palm factory, without knowing that Wis was locked up inside. He also conveyed the news that a number of the men who had attacked the police headquarters had been arrested and detained. But most of them, led by Anson, had hidden in the forest and the plantation. The young ones still seemed to be full of zeal. Wis asked: how is your wife and the other women? They were also detained at the police station. Apparently they were safe. They'd been helped by a lawyer from Legal Aid. The plantation fire had led to the whole case being reported in the newspapers. The Legal Aid people had found out and had come to see them.

Their pace was slowing down considerably. "And what about your own plans, Anson?"

But the young man was lost in his own thoughts. Wis also fell silent, it was all so complicated. The law would prosecute those who were considered to be the instigators. They were now fugitives. The people who had murdered Upi, raped Anson's wife, destroyed their windmill, uprooted their rubber trees – none of this would be relevant in the eyes of the judge. They would not even be brought to court. Wis sighed. He regretted having asked Anson about his plans at a time when the young men were feeling pleased with their successful torching of the factory. Thinking about the future would only serve to undermine that small victory. It would render their revenge meaningless. "Go into hiding for the time being, Anson. When I'm better I'll join you."

Wis didn't want to go to Perabumulih because he was afraid that the people who had interrogated him would be spying on the parish house. It would be dangerous for Anson, for his friends and for himself, not to mention the Church. He asked to be taken to the Boromeus nunnery in Lahat. That was where he parted company with Anson and his friends. He embraced the young man who knelt at his bedside.

"Don't get caught, Anson. I'll come looking for you as soon as I get out of here." However in truth he had no idea of what he would do; what would happen to Anson – and to the other detainees, to the women – while he just lay here in hospital.

"I know you'll recover quickly. God has come to your rescue so many times," the young man said, squeezing Wis's arm as he left.

But Wis said nothing. He just thought to himself, No, Anson. It wasn't God. If it was God, why didn't He save Upi.

The examining doctor estimated it would take him two or three months to recover. He had a concussion, his bladder had been injured, a number of his internal organs were bruised, his jaw, nose and almost all the bones in his fingers were broken, and his nerves had been damaged by the electric shocks so that sometimes his body went into convulsions.

The surly Sister Marietta regularly brought the newspaper to him, along with clippings of earlier news reports. She had been a high school teacher for a long time and treated him like a schoolboy. In the newspapers he read about the things he'd been accused of. The Head of Police Intelligence in South Sumatra made reference to an intelligent provocateur behind the resistance of the Sei Kumbang villagers: *There is evidence that the prime mover behind this action is a man of the cloth who has taken on some left-wing views.* He was accused of inciting the Lubukrantau villagers to obstruct development – *the development of palm oil plantations must be given absolute priority because it is our most important non-fuel commodity.* He was also accused of promulgating liberation theology, and of pitting the company against the farmers in order to create instability. But they only referred to him by his initials: AW.

Father Westenberg visited him secretly, but he was unable to come often. He was sure he was being spied on. After about a week, when Wis was starting to feel stronger, Father Westenberg spoke to him, his voice restrained and his green eyes calm. He told him that a day before he found out that Wis was in Lahat, a letter from the police had arrived at the parish house. Athanasius Wisanggeni was a witness and a suspect in the case of the burning of the police station and the factory. "What do you have to say, Wis?"

Wis looked at the old man for a moment then shifted his gaze to the window frame. "Why has the letter only just come? After the fire? Why wasn't I accused after the first attack?" he said softly. He thought for a moment, and then asked, "What did you say to them?"

"I said I didn't know where you were. Because I didn't."

"Have they been told now?"

Father Westenberg shook his head. "I believe you have been subjected to unfair treatment. Besides, you're still unwell. I haven't told a soul. Neither have the nuns."

"What do you think, do they know that I'm safe, or are they

looking for some sort of indirect confirmation that I died in the fire? Because I didn't think anyone saw me escape that night." I don't even know how I got out myself.

Father Westenberg was still shaking his head. "The thing is, they were quite polite and didn't ask to search your room."

Wis fell silent again.

"Does the Bishop know?"

"Yes, he's heard. He's sent a special team to investigate the matter."

"What do you think will happen, Father?"

Father Westenberg sighed, and then with apparent difficulty replied: "If the team can be convinced that you're not guilty, then you'll have to comply with the police request. If you yourself feel that you are guilty I think the best thing would be for you to step down from your pastoral responsibilities. After that it will be up to you whether you hand yourself in or not."

"It's not fair, Father. Both options represent a form of punishment." But his throat became constricted before he could finish what he had to say. In his current condition, the slightest emotion was enough to send a convulsion through his body.

His colleague stroked his head, moved at the young man's plight. "Don't worry about it too much, son. I'll think of something for you. But you, or should I say we, can't hope for too much from the hierarchy. The Church itself is in a compromised position. The congregation is frightened by the spectre of Communism. The accusation of forcing people to convert to Christianity can only bring us into disrepute." And these are the things of which you've been accused.

The two men fell into silence. Sister Marietta, who had joined them, was silent too.

Wis said to them, "I really don't think they know I'm still alive."

A few days later a car took Wis from the hospital to a location known only to the five nuns and a doctor. The Bishop wasn't informed. The Church hierarchy only heard that Father Athanasius Wisanggeni had disappeared. Some believed he had died in the factory fire. And Father Westenberg, who was constantly besieged by people, chose to say that he didn't know where he was. For the next three months or so Wis was nursed back to health.

And he changed his ID card for the duration of the trial, which went for about two years. He chose the name: Saman. He had no particular reason for this choice of name. It was just a word that popped into his head.

New York, 28 May 1996

My name is Shakuntala.

My father and my sister call me a whore because I've slept with a number of men and a number of women (even though I've never asked them to pay). My sister and my father don't respect me. I don't respect them.

For me, to live is to dance and dancing begins with the body. God gives breath on the fortieth day after a speck of flesh was formed by the union of egg and sperm, so the spirit is indebted to the body.

My body dances. Because dancing is an endless exploration through my skin and my bones, with which I feel pain, hurt, chill, pleasure, and – one day – death.

My body dances. It submits not to lust but rather to passion. Passion that is sublime, libidinal. Labyrinthine.

My name is Shakuntala.

I watch my friend Laila through the window. She emerges from the dust haze that's being blown about by the wind. She appears from below the pavement. First her head, then her body, then her legs, like a baby being born, emerging from the underground subway station. She's walking briskly, but the swirling dry leaves are chasing her, they eddy around the flea market in the empty lot, though all the vendors are packing up to go home. It's late afternoon. Five minutes later she comes into the apartment without the chiming of the lift's bell. The dilapidated old elevator is still out of order. She would have used the stairs.

I see the blank expression on her face, like a burning wick that's had a glass jar clapped over it. I don't ask her what's up because for sure she will tell me before too long.

She throws her bag onto the rug, and all her papers come flying out. Sketches. Poems. They flutter before the lamp, causing it to dim a little for a moment.

"He's dead. He's dead."

Her face is like a melting candle and I am afraid it might solidify into a mere clump of wax, no eyes, no mouth with which to communicate.

"Sihar didn't turn up?"

"He's been killed. I'm scared he's been killed."

"What?"

Then she reveals her theory that her lover has been killed by a hired hit man. Some brute out for revenge, or just someone from the military. I find this hard to believe. Not because it couldn't happen. I have read about Dietje, the model who was murdered outside the Kalibata rubber plantation, after her love affair with a politician. And about Marsinah, the factory worker who was tortured to death, so viciously that her uterus was crushed. It's just that I have never thought such a brutal thing could happen to anybody I knew. Murder is like an angel: it exists but it is utterly remote; it will never appear before me or any of my friends. But what is it that makes it inconceivable? And I start to believe Laila because I've never seen her so worked up before. She's shivering. It's true that New York in May is still chilly, but she's also as pale as a *cicak* lizard. (We don't have them here in New York.) I add some nonfat milk to a a cup of coffee I made for Laila. I'm of the belief that caffeine gets the blood circulating and milk calms the nerves. I'm also of the belief that once you get to thirty you should start cutting down on fat. Laila should go on a diet. She's getting quite chubby. There are folds of fat around her neck. She shouldn't be drinking full cream milk.

"Have you checked your story out?"

She shakes her head. "The people in his office wouldn't talk to me. Probably because they didn't want to be the ones to convey the bad news. Anyway, it's still too early there…"

"Tala," she turns to me again. "Help me, please. Phone his house in Jakarta for me, find out what's happening…"

I'm an expert at imitation. Sometimes I'm the Ramayana monkey-king Sugriwa, complete with low guttural growl. Other times I'm Cangik, whose slow, sluggish voice somehow seems to suit the flabby skin around her armpits. When I was a teenager I always used to dance as Arjuna in the *wayang orang* and all the girls would idolize me because, without realizing it, they saw no signs of femininity in me. But I was also Drupadi, who ignites the passion of all five Pandawa brothers. During my time in New York I've earned a reasonable amount of money on the side by doing voice-overs for experimental animated films. And if you've got the gift of tuning your vocal chords, just as you'd tune a radio, how hard can it be to do a male voice? Even though it isn't his wife who answers the phone, I've transformed myself into an American male. Afterwards I go over to my friend who's curled up on the sofa with two sketches and some seemingly random lines of verse: *I yearn for the hungry mouth / of a man whose youth is gone / left behind in the sand where he has sought his fortune.*

"Sihar's not dead," I say, a little disappointed. It's true, I am disappointed.

Laila looks at me, relieved and hopeful.

I go on: "He's in the Days Inn Hotel. 57th Street, West. With his wife."

Her face changes, something is withering away there, like a piece of rice-cracker being dipped into a bowl of hot soup. There's a flash of fighting spirit, then it fades. Of course she had been facing two equally painful possibilities: that he was dead or that he had let her down. The latter appears to be the case.

ॐ

What is the difference between dreams and reality?

It was 1975. My father sent me off to a strange new city. It was a vast place, like a jungle, so when I set off for school my mother always gave me two bread rolls. One to eat. The other to tear into little pieces so I could leave a trail of bread to follow on my way home. I learnt a lot from Hansel and Gretel. They had an evil father too.

The school I had been exiled to was housed in a very peculiar building surrounded by a river so deep that ancient fish inhabited its depths. Nobody knew how many of them there were; they had been there for hundreds of years and nobody had ever seen a dead fish floating on the water. The fins of these fish gave off phosphorescent glow as they swam in the dark crevasses and gullies of the river. But when they reached the surface of the water, their fins would get caught on the algae, sluggish and black with age, rather like a forelock of hair. They rarely surfaced and when they did it was only for a second or two, leaving a fleeting impression of ripples and shadow. Green water. Green moss.

The gates of the school could be raised and lowered with an iron chain that was greasy with oil. When it was lowered the steel-spiked wooden palings formed a bridge. When all the pupils were lined up ready to go in the principal would rotate the lever until the gate shut with a loud boom that made your hair stand on end. Any student trying to escape would fall into the river, and those ancient creatures would devour him with more relish than an eel eating a fat, fresh, warm turd.

I used to weep because I wanted to go back to my quiet little town. But there was no way I could escape. It was impossible.

And so I danced.

My body danced. It twirled and writhed like a flower bud cut by children from its stem and then set on a course in a stream. I saw them following me everywhere I went: children following their dancing flower bud from the dikes. When I had finished they would clap their hands.

"Hey new kid, where are you from?"

"I'm descended from the nymphs."

They laughed so hard it knocked me off my feet.

I am descended from the nymphs. I lived in a women's compound where all the children danced. All around the compound were hills inhabited by giants: the ogre with a protruding jaw, the ogre with flaming hair, the green ogre, the eggplant-nose ogre, the carrot-nose ogre, the radish-nose ogre. *Ferocious ogres.* They were both the enemies of and the butt of jokes by the knights, who dismissed them scornfully as weird, insignificant fugitives. But I fell in love with one of them.

Because the ogres would be killed as vermin if they set foot inside the compound, which was behind the knights' quarters, I used to meet him secretly under the *kepuh* tree. We wound about each other like a royal serpent Nagagini making love to a common snake. But the gardener caught us and told my father. He gave orders for the knights to capture my lover and I was exiled to this town. Here he would tie me to my bed at night and drill me in the first two rules of love. These were his lessons: *First.* It is the prerogative solely of the male to approach the woman. A woman who chases a man is a whore. *Second.* A woman shall give her body only to the right man, who shall support her for the rest of her life. That's what is known as marriage. Later, when I had grown up a little, I decided that marriage was nothing more than hypocritical prostitution.

In this alien city, every day at sunset my father would give the orders for me to be tied to my bed. Because I was descended from the nymphs. But what he didn't know was that each night I would learn to enjoy the pain. In the mornings I would take pleasure in stretching my limbs when the chains were taken off. During the day I did my lessons at school. Mathematics, science, social science, the state ideology Pancasila, and handicrafts.

The other students sneered at me and one by one began avoiding me. Only one girl would listen to what I had to say. I never knew if she believed what I said or just liked my stories. But she stood by me. Her name was Laila. She's been my friend ever since.

$$\wp$$

I look at her, my friend Laila. Her heart is like an onion: when the dry crispy skin is peeled off there is another layer beneath it, a layer that stings the eyes and makes you cry. Her eyes are telling me she is on the verge of tears.

"Why does his wife have to tag along with him everywhere?" she asks with restrained anger.

I try to console her: "Well it's what you would expect, isn't it? This is a chance for them both to have a holiday in America for the price of just one ticket."

She sighs. "Yeah. You're right."

But I'm not about to provide Laila with ready justifications for letting Sihar off the hook, which is what she always does in Jakarta. "He should have told you. You gave him my address didn't you? Why couldn't he have phoned?"

"Hmm, yeah, I suppose…but how could he phone if his wife's always hanging around?"

"So he has to go with her when she takes a shit does he?"

"Well maybe she's got very efficient bowels."

"She's lucky then. I have to sit there straining for ten minutes. Even though I eat fruit and vegetables regularly. But Sihar could have made out he was phoning the office, and rung here."

"But then your number would be recorded on the hotel bill. From the number she would know it was a local call, not a call to Odessa. What if she phoned here to check up on him?"

"Well he could call from a phone booth then! It's what people usually do anyway; calls from booths are cheaper than hotel phones. Surely he could figure out a way to do it! Is he stupid or just not serious about you?"

But Laila just sighs, longer and louder than before. She disappears into the pantry and washes out her cup, even though she hasn't finished her coffee. I shouldn't have been quite so hard on Sihar, because it implies that he doesn't really love her. It could be that he has in fact been unable to phone because, as Laila suggests, he simply can't get a private moment. Trapped by his wife. Feeling a bit remorseful, I take *Tickle-me Elmo* from under the pillow and tickle his waist. The red-haired doll giggles gleefully in his husky childish voice. "You knew, didn't you, that this Elmo doll sold out in a month. I was lucky to get one. Now you can only get ordinary Elmos in the shops." Laila just clears her throat as she dries her cup and hangs the cloth on the rack. She doesn't give a shit about Elmo. "Jim Henson's death was a blow to us all. But why hasn't somebody else run with the Muppet Show?" Now I'm doing Kermit the Frog. Laila smiles but only with her mouth. Her eyes remain unmoved. So I just shut up. I turn on the TV and, as if by magic, the corpulent Rosie O'Donnell appears on the screen. On this occasion she's ordered everyone in her talk show audience, herself included, to come wearing a G-string. The way everyone is sitting, you would think they had hemorrhoids. Oh, the joys of acting: who can prove a thing? Maybe none of them is wearing any underwear at all. "Does Sihar like girls in G-strings, darling?"

"How would I know? Things like that never even cross my mind!"

But she does manage a wry grin as she babbles on. Taking a bowl of kimchi from the fridge she calls to me, "Tala! It's possible, isn't it, that he didn't actually come with his wife?" She eats some pickled radish with her chopsticks but my guess is she would rather be eating *rujak.* "Are you sure it wasn't his wife who answered your call?"

"It was a man, I told you!" I'm sure but then I start to have my doubts. "Unless his wife can do voices like me. But why would she need to do that?"

"Well maybe she knows about our plans."

"And?"

"And she wants to wreck them. Or at least lead us into some kind of trap."

"But why? Besides, if that were the case then Sihar would have no excuse at all not to call you."

Laila pulls a grim face. "Yes, you're right…What's he afraid of? I don't want to upset his wife. I just want to see him. I don't want to disturb his family…"

I'm quiet for a while.

"Or," I say, trying to console her, "maybe he doesn't want to hurt you." *Because you're still a virgin.*

㊖

When I was nine I was not a virgin. People didn't consider a girl who didn't yet have breasts to be a virgin. But there was something I was keeping secret from my parents:

When they got wind of the fact that I was secretly meeting an ogre, my mother revealed a big secret: that I was actually made of porcelain. Statues, plates and cups made from porcelain come in hues of blue, light green, even brown. But they mustn't be allowed to crack, because if they do they will be thrown on to the rubbish dump or used as tombstone ornaments. My mother said I would never crack as long as I kept my virginity. I was taken aback: how could I preserve something I didn't yet have? She told me that there were three openings between my legs. Don't ever touch the middle one, she said, because that's where it's kept. Later I was disappointed to discover that I wasn't unique; I wasn't the only one who was special. All girls were the same. They might only be teapots, bowls, plates or soup spoons, but they were all made of porcelain. And as for boys? They were ivory: and all ivory cracks. When I grew up I found out that they're also made of flesh.

When my parents discovered that I was going out with an ogre from the forest, they gave me their second piece of advice. Virginity is a woman's gift to her husband. And virginity is like a nose: once you lose it, it can't be replaced. So you must never give it away before you get married, because then you will be damaged goods. But the day before I was sent to this foreign place I made a decision. I would give my virginity to my lover the ogre.

On that last night, under a purplish moon, I crept out to the pavilion and tore it out with a teaspoon. It looked like a red spider's web. I put it in a wooden Jepara box and gave it to the dog. He was in fact a courier between me and the ogre.

"What did it feel like the first time?"

"I didn't feel anything."

"Didn't it hurt?"

"It didn't hurt me."

"How come?"

"I don't know. Maybe because I'd never experienced any trauma about it."

"What do you mean, trauma?"

I discovered a long time ago that for me to live is to dance. Not on a stage but in a room inside myself. I don't have a sense of whether that room has walls or not, but it's a retreat, a place where nobody else can go. It's a place where I dance without music. Oh, the music is there, I can hear the *roceh* and the *rebab*. But it is playing quite independently of my dancing. We're quite self-sufficient, the music and I, we don't feel the need to complement each other and we definitely don't want to be called upon to perform for the sultan or the tourists visiting the palace. Maybe there are a few people out there; one by one they come to watch, but I have no interest in them, and neither do the gamelan players. I dance as a way of celebrating my body. But the crowd thinks I'm part of their entertainment. This causes problems. They clap their hands and call me The Dancer. Then they build a stage in the town square and hang kerosene lamps all around, and they explain that The Dancer should be curvaceous and voluptuous in order to please the audience, she mustn't detract from her femininity by being too energetic, and she mustn't be too languid or they'll fall asleep. So what happens is that she becomes little more than a hired performer who sways her hips and performs the *tayub* dance or the *ronggeng* dance on demand. They're all crazy about her. The Dancer is no longer celebrating her body. It no longer belongs to her. Just as a wife no longer possesses her own body. So that's the reason I always return to that room inside myself, where the dancer and the musicians perform solely for their own pleasure.

"Vaginismus. I once heard about a woman who couldn't have sex. Her vagina would close up every time a penis came anywhere near it. She had a deep subconscious fear of her own sexuality. She was at one extreme, I'm at the other."

Laila chortles. "Hey, what if that's my problem too?"

I laugh too. "Just imagine it. He's finally managed to sneak away from his wife to meet you. And you're ready for it too. But when the moment comes he can't get it in.

"Hey Laila, have you heard the story about the ignorant honeymooners? They were doing it in the dark. The husband was having a very difficult time trying to deflower his wife. When he eventually managed to do it, exhausted and relieved, too, that she was clearly a virgin, it turned out that she hadn't taken off her underpants and what he had deflowered was actually her panties…"

But Laila has stopped laughing.

"Are you convinced he's here with his wife?"

I stop laughing too.

"Are you sure that you'll actually do it if you do get together with Sihar?"

She shakes her head. "I don't know. What do you think?"

"I don't think you should."

"Why not?"

"It would be best not to."

I don't like Sihar.

When my dear friend got back from Sumatra two years ago she called me to tell me she had fallen in love. And what sort of genie has taken over your heart this time? I asked. A married genie apparently. This immediately became the main topic of conversation of myself and our two other friends, Cokorda and Yasmin. Laila was quite different from me or Cok, neither of us give a damn about marriage or hell, apart from a mutual belief that both of them are institutions. Laila was on a mission to find a suitable man with whom she could make a family and please her parents. Two acts of devotion that would no doubt bring their own rewards. It sounded lovely. Even I would like that.

But finding a husband is like finding a dining suite that suits both your room and your finances. We venture forth with our specifications and our budget. On the other hand a lover appears out of the blue like a painting that unexpectedly captures our heart. We simply must have it and we redesign the whole room to suit it. Laila was always falling in love with paintings instead of dining tables. As a teenager she fell in love with a young Catholic guy. He joined the priesthood and went away. She was obsessed with him for ten years; she would send him poems all the time, even though he was no doubt engrossed in tending to his flock. And now she's begun a saga with a married man. You're not going to be able to marry him either, we warn her. But I love him, she says. Yeah, yeah.

There's nothing wrong with love. It fills up something that wasn't empty in the first place.

But what was happening in this case was romance, which empties something that was shallow in the first place and fills it with longing. And lust. I never did know if Laila knew the meaning of lust. Her relationship with the priest seemed to be genuinely platonic. It wasn't until her fifth semester at school that she dated a guy who would stroke the nape of her neck and her ears. I was always asking what he did to her. "He kissed me," she said one morning. "Well don't let it happen again," I said. "From now on you have to be the one to kiss him. And did it make you wet?" I asked. "I don't know," she said. "Is that the same as a discharge?"

Now she's going out with someone else's husband. A man used to regular sex. Cok and I made a bet with Yasmin that there was no way he would be content with hugging and kissing. The loser of the bet had to go to the drugstore at Sogo department store and buy a packet of condoms – the ones with bumps all over them like bittermelons. The purchase had to be made at the busiest time of the day, to ensure maximum embarrassment. Yasmin believed that a man could love someone without having to screw them. Of course he can, I replied, he can love his child or his dog. And this guy doesn't have either. Sure enough, eventually he took Laila to a motel. Laila phoned me beforehand. "I think he's going to find us a room, but I don't know where yet. Tell the others. If anything happens, I'll be depending on you." "Okay," I replied, feeling a bit stressed out. "Give me a call as soon as you get there." I rang Yasmin and Cok on their mobiles. We all began to feel tense, like intelligence agents planning a war.

Fifteen minutes later the phone rang. "I'm at the Copa Cabana," she whispered. "Sihar's in the bathroom. I'll call again later. He doesn't want me talking to my pals about this." She hung up before I could say be careful. We love you.

I immediately called Yasmin and Cok. And we were all nervous, not about who would have to buy the knobbly condoms of course, but worried that something might happen to Laila. What that something might be I didn't really know. I sat by the phone for the next two hours.

"Tala?" Her voice was still subdued.

"Laila! Hi…did you do it?"

"Do what?"

"It…"

"No. Not properly."

"But you came?"

"He did."

"What about you?"

"I don't know…tell the others I'm okay." Click.

All three of us were so relieved. There remained the problem of the condoms. Yasmin was adamant that she didn't have to buy them because intercourse hadn't actually taken place. "You can't get out of it that easily," I insisted. "The bet was whether or not they would have sex." "But they didn't have sex!" retorted Yasmin. "Says who? The bottom line is, any activity that results in mutual arousal or that stimulates the sexual organs counts as sex. Especially if they reached orgasm. The issue of whether or not he put it in is a mere technicality." Neither of the others could deny that masturbation constitutes a sexual activity. And who's to say that Laila wouldn't be able to get pregnant as a result of what they had done?

And less than a month later Laila was saying her period was late. I shared her concern, because these days you can hardly get away with Kunti's story of the Hindu priest who helped her give birth to Karna through her ear so that her hymen wouldn't be broken, though I have always been curious about what Kunti must have looked like when the baby was passing through her neck. "I'm scared," said Laila, ashen-faced. "But you do know, don't you, that conception doesn't take place in the stomach or intestine, so you don't have to worry if you swallow it?" "I'm scared." "Have you told Sihar?" "He says it's impossible." "Have you asked him to go with you for a test?" "He says it's impossible." "And what if you are pregnant?" "He says it's impossible." Yeah, yeah. We quizzed her about the position they used, but Laila was too embarrassed to go into detail. She was also too embarrassed to have a urine test at the lab. In the end Yasmin offered to take in a sample using her own name. We waited in the car with the air conditioning going full blast because Laila was sweating like a pig. Half an hour later Yasmin returned with a negative result. We celebrated by feasting on noodles from a portable stall parked outside our old high school, Tarakinata Puloraya, remembering the days when we were still young, still virgins. Well, Laila still is a virgin. And now that we were grown-up, the noodles tasted disgusting.

"If you go out with him a couple more times, are you still going to be able to hold out on him?" "I don't know. Yes, I have to," she replied. But for months after that I didn't hear another word about Sihar. What happened, Laila, did you let the genie out of the bottle before he granted you your three wishes?

"He bought me three books that I'd been asking for, in Singapore."

"And you've given him five CDs, a book about testing children's intelligence, a book on gynecology and sent lunch to his office on three separate occasions: from Pizza Hut, Hoka-hoka Bento and Bakmi GM."

"You're crazy! You're so stingy. You have to balance the books on everything."

"You're too nice. I'm worried that you're too good for him."

But that's Laila, she's generous to everybody. She's the best friend I've ever had. That's why I worry she'll get hurt. Maybe I'm too protective?

I don't like Sihar.

I only met him three times in Jakarta before I got the grant to go to the States. He certainly fitted Laila's taste in men: athletic, dark-skinned, bespectacled, even-tempered, some grey hair, and a distinctive odor – tobacco, or sweat. To my mind he was too serious, lacking in imagination, slow at picking up humor so he was always the last to laugh – sometimes he had no idea at all of what the joke was about. Sex with him would most certainly be unimaginative and there would be no interesting post-coital conversation. But that wasn't what bothered me, although I didn't really know if I had the right to be bothered by anything. I knew they had been involved in some romantic adventure in Perabumulih: Laila, Sihar, Yasmin and Wisanggeni, the guy who had become a priest. I heard he had changed his name but I have forgotten what he calls himself now. But once Rosano had finally been cornered I got the impression that Sihar lost interest in Laila. The phone calls and dates became less and less frequent. He became elusive and difficult to contact. I was worried that he had simply been using Laila in his campaign of revenge. And now he had abandoned her and left her in a state of confusion over her new-found sensuality. I knew she was becoming bitter about her intangible erotic memories. Memories of seduction without orgasm.

But no. He hadn't just disappeared into thin air. He would suddenly pop up like a kid with a kite who knows that the west wind is beginning to die down. Just when Laila was sick of trying in vain to contact him, he would phone her out of the blue. Then they would arrange to meet somewhere but he would cancel at the last minute because something suddenly cropped up. My dear friend would be left stranded with her hopes still high. At times like that she would often ask me or Cok or Yasmin to phone Sihar. Of course mostly she asked me because I could disguise my voice. That was how I got the impression that Sihar was being deliberately evasive. One day his receptionist greeted me with: "Is this Agus from the insurance company or is it Laila's friend?" I was furious. How could some telephone operator know that I was looking for Sihar on Laila's behalf! No doubt he'd been regaling them all – the other office staff, the receptionists, the secretaries – with stories about Laila. He had probably told them that a girl called Laila Gagarina was chasing him, leaving out the important detail that he often called her as well. And no doubt when he got home from his rig in the South China Sea, he would tell his friends in that cool calm way of his, but with an undertone of maliciousness, "You remember that photographer chick who came here that time?" And he would tell them what she looked like after he had taken her clothes off as if he was talking about a bonus he had earned for finishing a job ahead of schedule, and they would all be ogling the girls at the bar in the belief they could be won over by money and big pecs, oblivious to the fact that these women had already subjugated them with their firm asses and their sweet talking. Bastards.

I don't like Sihar. But my friend does. "Forget him, Laila." But she didn't want to forget him. I had nothing else to say.

"Do you want me to phone him at his hotel?" Because the phone still hasn't rung.

She has a bewildered expression on her face, like someone from the country trying to cross the street in Jakarta. If I phone him it means I'm denying him the chance to phone Laila first, extinguishing Laila's hope of being telephoned first. That could be interpreted as a sign that Sihar is avoiding her. And that would make her curl up inside. It would be like waking her up just to tell her that the lizard shit that fell on her lips is not a nasty dream. I shut up. I let her wallow in her own thoughts.

❦

I have become increasingly skeptical of the notion that most ogres originated in India; rather, they boarded ships from Europe seeking spices in the East Indies. They had matted hair and sun-ripened skin because from the West the sun baked their bodies on the decks. And the salty air. These infidel ogres were accompanied by their priests, who were also infidels and ogres, and in the islands of Java and Bali they met brown maidens dancing naked in the river. Girls and older women bathing and washing. In fact slim brown men also bathed naked in the rivers, but their eyes only beheld what was chosen not by the eyes.

I could not possibly know what was in the minds of the ogres if I had not acquainted myself with one of them, who ventured deeper into the interior and spied on me dancing without a thread on my breast in a ditch by the hills. But I knew what was lurking, and because of that I sat down on a rock. Then he emerged from the clump of leaves and confronted me in amazement because I did not gather a cloth to cover my breasts.

"Who are you?" he asked.

"People here bathe twice a day," I replied.

Then he sucked the tip of my breast, unendingly, and told me his story. It was the first time he had sailed so far east. So far that he did not believe he could return to the West, even as the seas made you believe that the earth is round. In this country people thought that those in the East lived according to strange customs. Their men attached decorations to their penises, on the surface or within the skin. Their women, without shame, aroused the desire of their men and also of strangers, since they indulged in sex without any sense of taboo. Then he handed me a journal: IN THE LAND WHERE OUR LORD IS NOT YET KNOWN THE RACES WORSHIP THE LEWD. THEY CREATE MANY CONCOCTIONS FROM ROOTS IN A CAULDRON PURELY FOR CONTEMPTIBLE PLEASURE, ERECTING STATUES OF BODILY UNION. AVERT YOUR GAZE IF YOU BEHOLD THEIR WOMEN BECAUSE THEY POSSESS POWERS OF MAGIC. THEIR MEN ARE FORCED TO MUTILATE THEIR GENITALS WITH TERRIFYING OBJECTS – BEADS FROM BONES AS WELL AS THE FURS OF ANIMALS – TO FULFIL THE THIRST OF THEIR WITCHES FOR INCUBUS. BECAUSE THERE IS NOT A SINGLE BEING IN THIS WORLD WHO POSSESSES A PENIS AS LARGE AS THE DEVIL'S. THE GIRLS BARE THEIR BREASTS WITHOUT SHAME, SUSPENDED LIKE TWO PAPAYAS, A FRUIT THAT I WILL BRING BACK TO EUROPE FOR ALL OF YOU. THE SKIN OF THAT FRUIT IS SOUR. BUT ITS FLESH IS SWEET. SEEDS LIKE NIPPLES. (V D C, SERVANT OF OUR LORD WHO JOURNEYS, 1632)

I double up with laughter.

"Why?" he asked, "didn't you possess me with your nakedness? And your breasts are like chocolate milk."

Then he removed his trousers. Then I knew that the sun had baked his waist, chest and arms. And I told my story:

In this country people speak of your land and our land, your people and our people. We are the noble people of the East. You, the depraved of the West. Your women wear bikinis in the streets and have no regard for virginity. Your school children, boys and girls, live together out of wedlock. In this country sex belongs to adults through marriage even if they were married at the age of eleven and regarded as already mature. In your country people have sex on television. We do not have sex on television. We have the decent foundations of the great East. Your customs of the West are not noble.

Then I handed him a copy of the newspaper that I had used to wrap my panties. It reported on the opinions of bureaucrats about the danger of Western culture through films and consumer products. And also tourists on Kuta Beach. *Kompas*, 1995.

He looked bewildered. "Where are we?"

I said, "Aren't we in the 20th century?"

He was still puzzled. "This is a very strange place. How could I possibly be in two eras at the same time?"

I said, "Time is a curious thing. How can it separate us from the us of the past?"

And East-West is surely a strange concept, since we were discussing decency while stark naked.

※

I can't remember whether that was my first meeting with the ogre. Many things are easily forgotten, just as we completely forget why we can't remember them. Something can suddenly evaporate from our memory, like a ghost, like a dream. We can feel the trace of it, somewhere within ourselves, without being able to reconstruct it anymore. We are left with hatred, anger, fear, love. But we don't know why.

After my meeting with that ogre at that particular point, I did not only fall in love. Since that day I was full of dreams about their country. I wanted to see the land of the giants, to see their grand houses, their roads, their mice and their cats. Especially so I could get away from my father and sister, whom I had never respected, and they neither liked nor respected me. I didn't like them either. But the first time I went to get a visa from the Dutch Embassy, they asked me my surname.

"My name is Shakuntala. Javanese don't have surnames."

"You have a father, don't you?"

"If only I didn't."

"Use your father's name," said the woman at the counter.

"And why should I?"

"The whole form must be filled in."

I was livid. "Madam, you're Christian aren't you? I'm not, but I learned at a Catholic school that Jesus didn't have a father. Why does a person have to use her father's name?"

So I didn't go ahead with the visa application. Why should my father continue to own a part of me? But nowadays the Javanese have started to imitate the Dutch customs. A married couple gives the father's name to their baby, assuming that the child is glad or lucky to have been born. How misguided. How naïve.

In the past we were allowed to choose our own names. Grandmother called my father Timin. Just before he took up his lecturing job he began calling himself Mintoraharjo. My mother never changed her name because she liked the one she had been given. She was descended from Javanese nobility and from the nymphs who sing. But nowadays the court records your name at birth on an official document and you are cursed with it for life. Why should I take on my father's name? What about my mother's name?

So I didn't get to go to the land of the giants. I chose not to go. I was brokenhearted. However, later another opportunity beckoned from the West. From people in the West with an ever-growing interest in the people in the East, no longer because of their spices but because of something much harder to define – would you call it an interest in beauty, in diversity, in preservation? The Asian Cultural Center gave me a scholarship to explore dance. I would stay in New York for a couple of years, study dance and choreography at a number of festivals there, take part in a series of workshops, teach, and the highlight would be producing my own work. I would dance, and I would dance a long way away from my father. What joy.

Then I negotiated so that they did not force me to use my father's name on the papers. After all it wasn't part of our custom. And I thought it was unnecessary. "But a person can't have just one name," they said. Or maybe I wasn't a person? So I had to compromise, because even though I may not in fact be a person, I really wanted to visit their country. *First name*: Shakun. *Surname*: Tala.

♯
♪

Before King Charles II of England named it New York, the city was called Niewe Amsterdam. Novum Amsterdamum.

1625. The United West Indies Company established their first trading office there. Governor General Peter Minuit then bought the surrounding land from

THE INDIANS EVEN THOUGH THEY DID NOT THINK OF OWNING THE LAND AS PROPERTY THAT COULD BE BOUGHT AND SOLD. HE PAID THEM WITH TRINKETS AND ESTABLISHED A CORRUPT AND DICTATORIAL COLONIAL GOVERNMENT. HE WAS EVEN RUTHLESS TOWARDS HIS FELLOW WHITE MEN, AND THEY GREW TO HATE HIM SO MUCH THAT THEY SIMPLY SURRENDERED WHEN THE BRITISH WAR SHIPS ARRIVED. 1664. IN THOSE DAYS THE SAILORS WEREN'T YET WEARING CAMOUFLAGE OUTFITS, BUT WERE DRESSED IN COLORFUL UNIFORMS THAT LOOKED LIKE BANNER FISH.

THE DUTCH SHIPS HAD ACTUALLY DISCOVERED NEW YORK IN THE SEARCH FOR NEW TRADE ROUTES TO THE SPICE ISLANDS IN THE ORIENT. THE DUTCH TRADING CARTEL IN THIS PART OF THE WORLD HAD ITS COUNTERPART THAT HAD EARLIER EXPLORED THE FAR EAST: THE UNITED EAST INDIES COMPANY, VEREENIGE OOST INDISCHE COMPAGNIE (VOC), WHICH HAD BEEN ESTABLISHED SEVEN YEARS AFTER A MERCHANT AND ADVENTURER, CORNELIS DE HOUTMAN, HAD LANDED IN BANTEN IN JUNE 1596. THE VOC STAYED IN INDONESIA FOR 350 YEARS. BY THE NINETEENTH CENTURY THE INDIANS HAD DISAPPEARED FROM NEW YORK, AND THE INDONESIANS RECLAIMED THEIR POWER IN JAKARTA. (TOURIST GUIDE)

I arrived not by ship, those days are gone. But the world is indeed round. It rotates clockwise if we imagine ourselves standing in the South Pole looking to the other pole. And if we were in the North Pole it would rotate in the opposite direction. Weird, eh? Time is surely a curious thing, as I was in the plane for more than twenty-four hours, yet I arrived in America on the same day. I left on Thursday, didn't I, and now it's still Thursday? The earth is a phenomenon both round and miraculous.

But here winter has crept up on the city. Like dry ice, it glides from behind the buildings.

Then I discovered that New York is not the land of giants. But I wasn't disappointed, because I was a long way from my father. I knew that New York was an amazing place the minute I stepped into the subway. I would call it the *metro, memedi trowongan*, the shrieking ghost of the tunnel, because of the terrifying noise it makes as it weaves its way through the dark passages among the roots of the buildings. I observed the beings inside it. Sophisticated and uncouth. Skin as dark as ebony to complexions as light as a transparent sheet, so I could see the veins inside. If they took their clothes off their stomachs would surely remind me of clear plastic Swatch watches. The screws and levers would display as they moved. And we would be able to observe the process of separating food nutrients from bodily waste, without the smell. These people don't need X-ray or ultrasound machines. Just the doctor's naked eye.

Like a street urchin I emerged above ground on Sixth Avenue, and when I saw the long, straight avenues of Manhattan crisscrossed by shorter streets I felt like a rat trying to find its way out of a maze. The constant frenetic activity on the streets only intensified my confusion. Hordes of people hustling back and forth, under the lights, as varied as shoe sizes. People appearing from and vanishing into the vaporous city haze created by the heat of street lighting. A mélange of people, from the biggest to the smallest I had ever seen. At first I was disoriented by it. Had I landed in a Lilliputian land that Gulliver's people had colonized? Or was this in fact the land of Gulliver, who had gathered all the Lilliputians and presented them as an offering to his king, just as Christopher Columbus had taken the Indians to Madrid, where they'd bred like rabbits? Or were all these people like me, just here for a short time? Or were some here permanently and some just passing through? Were they all on grants?

At number 1209 a super-fast lift took me to the 34th floor. The office of the Asian Cultural Center. There was a round table and big windows, rather resembling the legs and ears of an elephant. From here I got my first bird's-eye view of New York. Far off to the right I could see the Empire State Building, the very first skyscraper, its pinnacle giving off a pomegranate-like glow. To the left – the Chrysler Building with its silver-pointed art deco tower. Down below I could see the skating rink in front of the Rockefeller Centre. It was frozen over and people were scuttling about like baby mice. So many of them. So diminutive. Distance renders people small and insignificant, as if you could simply squash them underfoot.

I've often suspected that grants have their genesis in some sort of guilt. Not that guilt is a bad thing. The towering building I was in seemed to be infused with remorse. In the massive lobby there was a triptych of murals depicting toiling laborers, in much the same way that capitalism romanticizes the proletariat, thus neutralizing any sense of exploitation. This is a prosperous city. Why then do people here fund foreign artistic projects that can't attract any money in the country they come from? Are they like the Renaissance men who, bored with the middle ages, re-discovered the Greek ruins and assiduously began to excavate them? Or does it derive from a feeling of guilt about centuries of Orientalism, hundreds of years of wealth obtained through colonialism? But suddenly I didn't really care. A work of art doesn't need to have its origins in just one emotion. It's like the mouth of a river, part of which is contaminated by pollution, by dead bodies even. I met a number of people. A few of them were program coordinators, a few were artists, a few were researchers, a few were grant-holders like me.

Each program has its own way of awarding scholarships. I was given a housing allowance and I was free to find my own place to live. Because I knew I would be going back to Jakarta before too long I decided to save as much money as I could. What seems like a pittance here goes a long way in Indonesia. One dollar was worth two thousand five hundred rupiah. I rented an apartment in Chelsea that was well within my budget, in an alleyway with graffiti-covered walls, tucked in behind a pawn shop and a second-hand cassette shop where I could get three CDs for two dollars. It reminded me of Jakarta where the hawkers would set up their stalls on the verandahs of the department stores and loudly proclaim their bargains: three pairs of underpants for a thousand rupiah. I never bought any because I don't always wear them. They make me prone to infections. In humid tropical climates I think women are better off not wearing underwear, unless they are menstruating. But here in winter I need them for warmth and to prevent me from catching cold.

Compared to those of my acquaintances – Mei Yin, Abby Chan, Araya and the others – my apartment is the worst. The lift is often out of order and the neighbors' cooking smells linger in the corridor. You are allowed to keep pets here, and my neighbor is forever losing her cat, but that doesn't prevent her from going out and getting another one. But I'm never lonely; I live in an alleyway in Jakarta too and I have gone for months without a partner.

Before I left, my jet-setting friends said to me, "There's no city in the world with a more vibrant artistic spirit than New York." And as the days went by I came to discover how amazing this place really is: it is a melting pot of ever-creative performances that are never short of audiences. Only Dasamuka, with his ten heads, would be able to fully appreciate everything that's going on at the Lincoln Centre. But even then his heads would have to be able to go off on their own and come back to share their experiences. People on a family holiday can wander along sparkling Broadway and take in conventional local or imported musicals: *Phantom of the Opera, Les Misérables* (if you're not looking for a happy ending), *Beauty and the Beast* (if you are). But in my view *Beauty and the Beast* actually has a sad ending: after Beauty has fallen in love with the Beast, the monster changes into an ordinary man. But tucked away in the quiet nooks and crannies you can come across both actors and spectators who are so out there that they make the theater of the absurd look mainstream. This stuff will scare your children: from mystical music to whispered voices and bizarre tragedy. They perform in theaters in Off-Off Broadway that only seat seventy spectators, sometimes as few as ten. There are no permanent theaters for this type of performance in Indonesia. There are just the huge theaters, as if art must always be on a mass scale. I have danced in Jakarta before an audience of about forty people, but only in the homes of the wealthy or in art galleries. There are also those who dance naked and copulate before an audience of about forty people in hotels and the homes of the wealthy, and then get arrested. But it's all sporadic – the performances as well as the arrests. There's no building dedicated to such things. So here I spend all my spare time taking in shows and working on my own creative pieces.

I love it. It's like climbing a mountain and discovering a cauldron of experimental expression at the peak, and then plunging into it. I'm utterly content, even though people here call me Miss Tala when they wish to be polite and Shakun in less formal situations. Shakun – it sounds like *jakun*, meaning "Adam's apple" in Indonesian, or *kalkun*, meaning "turkey". I don't know what sort of permutations the Indians work on the name Shakuntala.

But my friend Laila is not happy in New York. And for good reason. She's walked out on a number of projects in Jakarta and blown part of her savings. She's not the sort of person who can afford to fork out two thousand dollars for an air ticket at the drop of a hat. On top of all that, there's no sign of the guy she's been waiting for in Central Park.

And he doesn't answer his phone.

I'm beginning to wonder if maybe it's a case of experience being a good, if cruel, teacher. Isn't Sihar always doing this, making an arrangement and then cancelling it at the last minute? That is why I was so pessimistic when Laila phoned me, full of optimism, a few months ago and talked about him, still the same as ever. I'm coming over, she said. We're going to meet in Central Park. *The place where people can be happy.*

"Laila, it's a huge park. Where exactly?"

"He said to wait near the statue of Columbus."

"Where will he be staying?"

"I don't know yet, he'll let me know."

I sighed. "So you're still captivated by him?" I asked, my tone a mixture of surprise and annoyance. "Obviously I am," she replied. "After his ambivalence towards you for so long?" "He has to consider his wife's feelings, you know. He's a man of principle."

"So what are you actually looking for? Not marriage, not sex."

"I just want to be with him."

"Laila, if you meet him here you'll do it for sure. Are you ready?"

"No, I don't know…"

"He'll ask for it for sure. What do you want?"

"I just want to be with him. I'm sick of having to hold back."

I sighed again. "Yeah, okay. I'm really pleased you're coming."

But I asked her to invite the other two: Cok and Yasmin. My reasoning was that if Laila was let down, or if anything happened to her, the four of us would all be here. We always had a lot fun when we got together, and that might cheer Laila up. And I also wanted them to see my performance at the Brooklyn Art Museum.

When I had left for New York I never thought for a moment that my friends would visit me here. America is twice as far from Indonesia as Holland. But as it turned out, in the same week as my phone conversation with Laila, my two old friends started making plans. They were from wealthy families and both of them were now earning good money. Yasmin worked in her father's office so she could easily organize her leave. And Cok ran her own business. Not being an employee, she could come and go as she pleased. We would stuck together for a long time, these two and I. Cok, my buxom friend, was always cheerful, always happy. When you were with her you always felt that life was wonderful, and that nothing needed thinking about too deeply or too seriously. There was no anger that was worth sustaining, such as my bitterness towards my father. And there was no such thing as love that lasted, like the enduring sweetness in a jar of jam. Everything was like a tomato: bright and fiery today, and withered in a few days time. And no fridge. She was coming to America, purely for pleasure, and she was bringing her new boyfriend with her. I had no idea who he was. I hadn't even met the previous one, the one she left for this one. "Well even Laila's got a boyfriend, why can't I?" she laughed. And Yasmin was the same as ever too, the exact opposite to Cok in many ways. Her parents had taught her from an early age to use her time productively. When she was in second grade her mother started sending her to ballet classes, piano classes, swimming classes and English classes, and she became very adept at all of them. She never had to do her homework before school. Sometimes she even did her school work at home, in advance. It was exhausting to talk to her because her broad general knowledge meant that she tended to dominate any conversation. And now she wasn't just coming to New York for a holiday. She had some business with the New York office of Human Rights Watch. Yasmin often took on cases of human rights violation and she sometimes referred to herself as an activist.

"Laila and Cok have boyfriends. How come you don't?" I asked.

"I just don't." she said sharply. That was all.

And it was true that I had never heard of Yasmin having a relationship with anyone apart from her husband. They'd been married for five years, after going out together for eight. Cok and I were always amazed that she could bear the monogamy. Cok had had forty boyfriends, and was still not satisfied. And as for me, I'd been with a number of people. Some I'd left, some had left me and now I didn't have anybody. Apart from my three friends.

⁂

We've been friends since sixth grade. Back then I was the tallest. Laila was the smallest. Yasmin was the smartest. Cok was the most flirtatious.

We became a gang from about the age of fifteen. And as is usually the case in a gang, we would always support each other. But, as is also usually the case in a gang, we eventually felt the need to create a mutual enemy in order to strengthen the bonds between us. So we sat in a circle in Yasmin's bedroom, the door locked to keep everyone else out, and we drew up a list of felons. Yasmin reckoned that our main enemies were our teachers. I wasn't so sure because I was convinced that our main enemies were our parents. Laila believed that men were the ones we should be on guard against. And Cok couldn't come up with an enemy. I knew that she was jealous of a girl in class 2C. But she couldn't put her on our list of enemies. The trouble was, Cok didn't know which of our suggestions she should vote for either. So we had a big debate.

What's wrong with teachers? I put the question to Yasmin and she answered: they give us too much work and they tell on us to our parents. They also punish and humiliate their students. Laila agreed. It's true, she said. If the teachers didn't give us so much homework we would have more time to play. But I chimed in: you're targeting the wrong people. If these are the issues, then the blame still lies with our parents, because they're the ones who enroll us in school.

What do you think Cok?

She nodded. "Yeah, parents are a pain. So are teachers. It's a tie."

But our parents love us and our teachers don't, Yasmin insisted. Our parents look after us, go out to work for us, give birth to us. But I persisted with my objections. I said: that's precisely my point! It's precisely because we were born that we have to go to school. Our parents are still to blame. If we hadn't been born, we wouldn't have to study. But on this point Yasmin and Laila promptly joined forces: religion teaches us to respect our parents, they said. This pissed me off. If one listened to the two of you, I said, invoking religion like that, then in the end God is to blame. This made Yasmin really mad and we nearly came to blows. Laila broke us up by suggesting we put the whole matter aside, because in her view men were the enemies. But suddenly Cok piped up to disagree. I knew that she had just started going out with a third-year boy.

What have men done wrong?

Laila replied: they betray women. All they want is a woman's virginity, and then they leave after she's given it to them. Just like it says in the song. We all sat there thinking. For a long time. A very long time. Suddenly I felt the urge to blurt something out but I kept my mouth shut because I didn't want to start another fight. What I wanted to say was that God was the one who had sold us short: he had created a hymen for the female but not for the male.

But, Yasmin eventually said, our fathers didn't leave our mothers, did they? Laila was at a loss for words for a bit but then she came up with her defense: our mothers didn't relinquish their virginity until after they were married. So that's why our fathers didn't leave them. As she spoke I clapped my hand over my mouth, because I was dying to say something else, which both of them would regard as blasphemy.

But a few moments later another brainwave erupted from my lips: "I know who our enemy is!"

"Who is it?"

Not God. "Our enemy is MY father! You see, he's a teacher, a parent and a man! "

But my great discovery only muddied the waters even further. And in the end we just had to agree that it was impossible to make an incontestable decision on who was the enemy, even though all three proposals could be used as criteria. But I didn't understand why they didn't want to adopt my father as the enemy. After all, he fulfilled all the conditions, didn't he?

As we got older it became increasingly obvious to Laila, Cok and me that our main enemy was our parents. By then time had wrought changes on our bodies. Our breasts had developed and Yasmin had become lithe and slender; she was the tallest now. Laila was still sweet, with a childlike innocence about her. The first time she fell in love it was with Wisanggeni, so of course she then threw out the notion of men being the enemy. At the time he was a seminary student, and one of his duties was to come to our school to lead classes in social awareness. Obviously he wasn't interested in taking her virginity. She was besotted with this ordinary-looking but kind-hearted guy, and she would fill her diary with the words "Brother Wis". On every page she would write it, a dozen times. But Laila was from a Moslem family of mixed Minang-Sundanese parentage. Her parents found the diary and she was in deep trouble. They were on the point of moving her to another school. At the same time Yasmin, who is Catholic, also disapproved of Laila's infatuation with the priest, because a priest must be celibate. (I kept mispronouncing the Indonesian word *selibat* as *sembelit*, which means "constipated".) But because the four of us had sworn an oath to stick up for each other, Yasmin was prepared to shelter Laila from her parents if she was desperate to see Wis. He understood that the emotions welling up in Laila's heart were as pure as milk being poured into a pot, and he would listen politely to her prattle. I had read Laila's diary myself and from it I gathered that she had no sexual interest in the male of the species. Her love was like devotion, a package comprising the desire to adore and to give. But meanwhile Cok and I were furtively exchanging tales of our own dalliances, comparing the erotic zones of the guys we were dating. Sometimes we would sketch them on paper. And we were beginning to discover that not all men are the same.

We lost Cok suddenly when we were in grade eleven. One day without warning her desk was empty. And a week went by with no sign of her, no goodbyes. The teachers were asking: where's the little vamp got to? We phoned her but nobody picked up. We were a bit reluctant to go to her house because we had lied so often to Cok's parents when she was out on a date somewhere. Maybe they had found out about all that. In the end, unable to bear the thought of losing our friend, we carried out a surreptitious investigation. With a pair of binoculars we kept watch on Cok's house from Yasmin's car, parked on the other side of Tanah Mas road, hidden by the coconut and banana peddlers whose stalls lined the slow lane. We saw her father come home from work, the maid open the door, smiling, everything seemed to be normal, so we were none the wiser. But the following week the teachers stopped asking us about Cok and I suspected that they had found out what had happened. So I asked my homeroom teacher: where's Cok gone? She answered: she's been moved to Ubud. But why the haste? Because she's been mixing in the wrong circles in Jakarta.

Finally a letter came from Cok. This is what she wrote: *Dear Tala…Mom and Dad found a condom in my bag…I'm only writing to you. You see Yasmin and Laila would be shocked if they knew about this. They might decide they want nothing more to do with me.*

But I couldn't keep this to myself while my friends were still so puzzled about her disappearance. So I told them.

I watched their faces. It was like putting a hot iron to newly-washed satin. It shrivels up instantly. Immediate scorch marks. The shock and concern on their stunned faces was almost tangible.

"Well what are you gawking like that for?" I asked, irritably. I knew they were shocked that Cok was no longer a virgin.

Finally Laila said: "What did I always say? Our enemies are men. A man ruined her."

I was somewhat relieved that she didn't blame Cok. But I retorted: "Why men? Her boyfriend didn't leave her, you know! It was she who left him, because mommy and daddy locked her up."

"But believe me, he'll soon find himself another girlfriend in Jakarta. Why would he think about Cok when he's already got everything he wants from her?"

I had no answer to this because I didn't know Cok's boyfriend all that well. Besides, was he the same as every other guy in the world, and are all guys the same? And in her following letters Cok told me that she was in fact dating someone else in Ubud. What about your lover in Jakarta? I couldn't put up with a long-distance relationship, she said, but I also couldn't put up with not having a boyfriend.

But as time went by her stories became more and more complicated, because she would mention so many names in her letters. She was dating several guys at once. I got dizzy reading about it. If there was too much to tell in one letter, the story would suddenly leap to the next episode, like a soap opera. Are you sleeping with all of them? No, she said. Just some of them. Do you date more than one person on the same day? Yeah, but not every day. What about your parents sending you to a remote part of the country so you could learn some morals? They have no right to get angry any more, she said. In fact sometimes they have to protect me from angry lovers that I've cheated on.

The upshot of the crisis with her parents was that Cok finished high school in Ubud two years after the rest of us. Then she came back to Jakarta to do a course in hotel management at the Sahid Jaya because she wanted to continue her mother's business. Later she opened some bungalows with a gallery and café on her family's land in Ubud and Sanur, as well as hotels in Sumatra and Java. When she came back to Jakarta we all resumed our friendship again. But we were all more grown-up than we had been three or four years earlier. After a war of words with my father, who just wanted me to be clever, I went to the Jakarta Arts Institute and continued to dance. Laila did a computer course at Gunadharma, but she loved photography too. And Yasmin got into law at the University of Indonesia without having to pass an entrance exam; she was snatched up by the university's talent scouts. But then the once pious Yasmin began to date men. Her wealthy parents bought her a house in Depok near the campus. On the weekends she would go home to her parents' place at Simpruk, from Monday to Friday she and her boyfriend would greedily explore each others' bodies. He eventually left his boarding house, with its musty smell of chickens, and moved in with Yasmin. It was then that Yasmin coyly told us that she had been sleeping with Lukas.

"But we're going to get married," she add hastily, to cover her feelings of guilt about illicit sex.

And marry they did, after Lukas had got a job as a civil servant, and after they had remained faithful to each during eight years of dating. Lukas Hadi Prasetyo is Javanese. Yasmin Moningka is Manadonese, but she agreed to go along with the highly ritualized Javanese wedding ceremony. She even agreed to wash Lukas' feet as a sign of a wife's devotion to her husband, something which doesn't occur in a Manadonese ceremony. "What do you want to do that for?" I protested. But she just got annoyed. "Well Jesus also washed the feet of his pupils. And anyway, you're Javanese!" I would have liked to regale her with a long argument about her Jesus and my Java. I wanted to tell her, for example, that Jesus washing his pupils' feet represents a reversal of roles, while the action of a Javanese wife symbolizes obeisance and powerlessness. There's no comparison between the two. But it was their special week, a week I didn't want to sully. So I just said, "If I could I would like to become a Manadonese."

We were chatting in the bride's room, waiting for the make-up person to come to trim her bangs, forming a pattern that reminded me of the forehead of a wild cat, and to paint branches on the tips of her eyebrows, like the forked tongue of a snake. She finally arrived with her big make-up box and shooed us away: "Off you go, virgins aren't allowed in here; you'll steal the bride's beauty!" So Cok and I chased Laila out, because she was the only one who was still a virgin.

Suddenly we were thirty. Cok had made peace with her parents long ago. Yasmin, having passed her law degree, no longer regarded teachers as the enemy. I still harbored deep resentment against my father. And as for Laila, I don't know if she still counted men as enemy number one. She had fallen in love a few times and had never hurt men in the same way that Cok used to and lied to her lovers. When Laila fell in love it was never half-hearted. If he happened to mention that he felt like some rib soup or some fried bean sprouts, or he liked a certain cassette or a CD or some other trinket, Laila would rush out and buy it. She would always give him a present on his birthday. She loved sending cards and letters and just words. It was the same with Sihar. (*I yearn for the hungry mouth / of a man whose youth is gone / left behind in the sand where he has sought his fortune.*)

Darkness has reached the western horizon. Laila is lying slumped on the couch in my apartment. Like the banana palm I bought by mail order that came in a cardboard box, she is looking a bit wilted from lack of sunshine. The phone has rung a few times, in the film on TV. But Sihar has made no contact. The stars look like the points of skyscrapers from some other universe, mingled with the lights of Manhattan that chew up millions of watts of electricity. "I need a cigarette," says Laila.

PERABUMULIH, 11 DECEMBER 1990

With my greatest respect,

I hope this second letter of mine also reaches you, Father.

I beg your forgiveness for having caused you so much pain. I know you love me and that as a consequence you have suffered greatly because of all that has happened during the past year. The newspapers have unjustly accused me, but I know that this has caused you a great deal more angst than it has me, just as I know that the suffering of Mary on the road to the cross was far greater than that of Jesus himself. Parents always bear twice the burden of their children's troubles. On top of all that, you had no idea where I was and you couldn't contact me. I'll do my best to send news as often as possible so you will know that I'm safe. I'll try to phone when I can. Please don't worry on my account.

The wet season arrived with a vengeance this month. The air is fresher now; the haze has lifted because the rain has washed away the smoke from the forest-clearing fires, but it's getting more and more difficult to get around because the change of seasons has caused mudslides that block the roads. I'm still leading a nomadic sort of existence. But there's no need for you to worry because the women who looked after me so well when I was sick are still watching out for me. They are so caring, when I was with them I kept thinking about Mother. Not because of their similarities, but rather because of their differences. Mother was so warm, so amiable, so beautiful, so mysterious. She could make anyone fall in love with her. Even the angels and the evil spirits could have been captivated by Mother I think, but it wasn't her fault. On the other hand the women who have been tending to me are unassuming, business-like, diligent, neat, disciplined. The thing they have in common with Mother is that they all really love me. Love finds a place in the hearts of all sorts of people. I have also been sheltered by a number of other people, in the cities as well as the villages, who have been so kind and who took me in even though they knew what the papers were saying about me. And people such as these always renew hope within me, in the midst of all my feelings of confusion and powerlessness.

When I am in the city I always miss the smell of the forest. The smell of wet earth and burning wood. The same aromas we used to smell when you would take me to see the new plantations that had been opened with credit from your bank – more than twenty-five years ago when the Javanese were still coming here as transmigrants. It amazes me, when I think back on all that, to realize that although I have grown up, although you're getting older and Mother has passed away, the earth is still the same as it always was, created and renewed continually by the creatures that live and die on its surface. Life is a remarkable thing.

Sometimes I feel discouraged when I think about the smokehouse I built with my friends, using the money you gave me. You have been so good to me. I owe you a huge debt of gratitude, even though nothing remains of my endeavors. There are still a few million rupiah in the bank, the remaining profits from the plantation, but we can't access it yet because we're afraid of getting caught when we try to withdraw it. A few days ago I had a surreptitious look around Lubukrantau and noticed a number of trucks laden down with polythene bags of young green oil palm seedlings, which had obviously been cultivated very diligently. There was a whole convoy of trucks from the seed-raising factories to the farmers' land. These oil palm trees have begun to replace the rubber trees. The stumps of the rubber trees I'd planted are gone completely, right down to the roots. These fine healthy oil palms would no doubt develop into a booming forest industry were it not for the fact they had their genesis in bitterness: forced cultivation by the local farmers and outrageous deceit and fraud.

I asked a friend if I could see the agreement the people had signed. He told me that the company had indeed duped the people, because the terms of the agreement were that the farmers would hand over their land to Anugrah Lahan Makmur in return for some financial compensation. It's too simplistic to view the issue as a class struggle, a battle between the company and the farmers. On both sides there are greedy opportunists out to make as much as they can out of the situation. I believe that the company wants to own the plantation in the interests of efficiency and ease of control. They set aside a sum of money to buy the land from the farmers, realizing that many transmigrants had in fact already sold off bits of their land to city folk or to smaller business interests, once they could no longer work it themselves. The waters became muddied when the people delegated by the company to negotiate the deals with the farmers did so in a dishonest and ruthless way (and the company either facilitated it or turned a blind eye to it). I'm sure that a lot of the company's compensation money was in fact used to bribe these delegates to engage in deception and bullying as a way of subjugating the transmigrants. But by the same token a number of villagers also got paid to exert pressure on their friends. In view of that I'm predicting major problems in the next five to ten years. Or else the repression will be even tighter, as the transmigrants try to reclaim their land. Because their understanding is that for the next ten years the company will rent their land from them and share the profits.

For that reason. Father, I once again ask for your blessing. I want to stay on here.

Father,

I know it's often been difficult for you to reconcile your own aspirations with the decisions I have made about my life. I remember when I decided to enter the seminary. I know it was a disappointment to you, as I was your only child, and my decision would mean the end of your line of descent. I forced you into a life of loneliness because there would never be any grandchildren to entertain you, as befits a man in his retirement. And then after Mother's death, I just left. I even asked to be sent here, meaning that yet again you were left alone.

Gradually you came to terms with my departure by consoling yourself with the knowledge that I had gone in order to tend my flock, to strengthen the Church, or to embark on a general humanitarian mission. In other words, my task was nobler than ensuring your happiness. But that wasn't what I in fact experienced. It was nowhere near as lofty as that.

What I did was not inspired by abstract ideas about God or humanity or justice. I have to confess that it was quite by chance that I was drawn into doing what I did, that I was drawn into making certain decisions. *It was all a coincidence.* When I first met the people of Lubukrantau, when I saw them and began talking to them, I suddenly became involved in their lives. I kept wanting to go back there, and every time I did I became more intensely involved. There is no more apt word than "committed" to describe my relationship with them and my feelings for them. Perhaps you could call it love – but I don't think that's precise enough.

I experienced that commitment as something simple yet very moving. I believe that the love of a man for a woman or of a woman for a man is also something that happens quite unexpectedly yet is extraordinarily empowering. It makes us want to surrender ourselves. Not as a sacrifice but as an expression of passion. It also gives us the strength to deal with all manner of things. (In this respect I'm grateful that that passion never reached its climax so I never had to experience its decline.)

As I was going through all that, all the explanations about humanity, all the theology I had learned, were suddenly not enough. Ever since I was a young boy I have admired the holy men who live their lives simply. Francis of Assisi. Ignatius Loyola. The men who lived the lives of paupers while the popes were drunk on the glory of Christendom. Paul devoted almost all of his letters to an explanation of the extraordinary power of love. But love – actually I prefer to qualify it with the concept of "commitment" – is an experience that can't be captured by words. It can't be contained within any one definition. Even Paul only succeeded in discussing its characteristics. But we can only use characteristics to recognize love. If we use them as a guide, we end up with a new axiom that says that love comes from outside the body of man, that it is something that is not experienced but rather applied. If we force holiness, or even simplicity, upon people we merely produce an oppressive inquisitor who leaves a dark stain on history. And that's why I don't believe that God works by presenting us with a stone tablet upon which are inscribed his ideas about himself and mankind. God works by giving us the capacity to love, and that transforms itself into a creative force within us.

Dear Father,

There is something I wish to say with this explanation, and I hope you won't be disappointed.

Perhaps that's why when we're taking Mass we consciously try to rediscover and relive the suffering of God, so that we can go on experiencing it. Internalizing it. Because you raised me in that tradition, the story of God's suffering has always moved me. If a story is told by way of argument and persuasion, it can never hope to convey successfully its central meaning. A story is an experience that has no other way of being expressed.

But not everyone was born into that tradition. The story is more than two thousand years old. With all the subsequent shifts in cultural beliefs, and all the mistakes that the Church itself has made, it is quite likely that the story will become irrelevant. But I believe that God makes the sun rise and the rain fall for all human beings. I don't think Jesus wanted to have a monopoly on love. Redemption is one thing, but the capacity to become committed and to love is within all of us. Father, if we believe that God transformed himself into a human being so that he could experience what it is like to be human, then we have to believe that He can transform himself into anything at all. We don't always have to fly the flag of the Church. The flag is not only the property of the Church.

Lately, when I have had to choose whether to stay in the Church or to be with my friends to whom I am committed, I have been leaning towards the latter. Again I beg your forgiveness. Having opened your heart to the idea of me becoming a priest, here I am deciding to leave the priesthood. Not to make you happy, but to pursue something that isn't even certain. I have to confess that I am more than a little apprehensive about what I should do. I'm currently in hiding. This may go on for another year or two, until a verdict has been reached about the detained Lubukrantau villagers. Once a court case is over, they usually give up pursuing any fugitives (the money has run out!). In any case, it's becoming harder and harder to prove that I was a provocateur. That means I'll be able to come out of hiding. So you can rest easy.

Father, again I beg a thousand pardons for your son who is so uncertain of himself. I'm in the process of lobbying a number of overseas institutions to help fund a non-government organization I'm hoping to set up with some friends. An NGO that can operate in the plantations. But I'm also keen to do something – what, I'm not yet sure – which can in some way provide funds to some of the Lubukrantau villagers who have been left with no land and no jobs. Would you be willing, yet again, to give me some money to supplement what we've still got in the bank?

(One of my connections will phone you this week. I can't mention his name, but you know him.)

Father,

How is Banun? She must have had her baby by now, hasn't she? Is it a girl or a boy? Can't we just suggest that she and her husband stay in our house? It's such a shame Mother is no longer with us. She would have been so eager to help care for the baby, and then Banun would have an excuse to stay in Pejaten: a new mother always needs an experienced mother around her. And then you wouldn't be lonely. But I still think it makes sense to try to persuade them to live with you for the time being. They can put the money they save on renting towards buying a house of their own. Especially since Duwi's office is in the Cilandak Commercial Estate, isn't it? Give my best wishes to them both, and a kiss for the baby.

Are you still doing your early morning work-out with the group? How are the bulbuls and the turtledoves and the bantams? If I may make a suggestion, I don't think it's a good idea to separate them just so they'll sing. It's true of course that they won't sing if they are in pairs, but the fact is that they want to mate. It's not fair to treat them like priests. Birds don't choose to live a celibate life like priests and nuns! And they've had the same mates since they were quite young. It must make them sad to be separated. Can't you and the birds share your time? What I mean is, for certain periods you give in and let them be together, and for other periods the birds give in and abstain from mating so they can sing for you. Of course it will be a bit tricky reuniting them with their proper partners. You might have to mark them in some way, or give them special cages. What do you think? I think you'll enjoy it.

Your devoted son,

Wisanggeni

From: Saman <wisang@ibm.net>
To: Yasmin <yasmin_moningka@hotmail.com>
Date: Sat, 7 May 1994 22:32:30 -0500
Subject: New York

Dear Yasmin,

Here's my first email from exile. I've just got my new addresses: saman@hrw.org (work) or wisang@ibm.net (home).

Here I am, finally, in New York. I landed at Kennedy on the afternoon of the 3rd. It was wet, cold, windy. It felt empty. All I had ever wanted from this country was to witness my very first fall. People wrote about the maple trees that turn glorious in October, their leaves changing into brilliant scarlet. But I'll have to wait a full six months for autumn. What a shame.

I encountered no problems with customs at the airport. Probably because I was on a domestic flight, having already entered the country through Los Angeles. All the customs officers in LA had bullying looks and seemed extremely suspicious. I suppose that's the kind of face that superpower countries must show all new arrivals who want in. (And it seemed to me, for the first few days, that every time I went to the market the cashiers were checking my money to see if it was counterfeit.) Despite the long queues, a number of bags were opened, and a person of color was taken off to a special interrogation room. It made me feel uneasy. I have to confess that the sight of anyone in authority is still enough to fill me with dread. I always assume that such a person is not there to preserve the peace but rather to disrupt it. You yourself once said something similar: that even the sight of a traffic cop makes you anxious that maybe they're after you because one of your lights is out or something. My sense of unease was heightened by my not having so much departed Indonesia as having escaped it. I wouldn't have found it amusing if US Customs had deported me because of some administrative red tape. Fortunately everything went well at immigration.

Ferouz, my Bangladeshi friend from Human Rights Watch, was at the airport to pick me up. We caught the free bus to the subway station nearest to Howard Beach – capitalism, it seems, can also provide clean facilities at no charge. From the outside the station looked like some sort of warehouse perched on its own in a sea of cars left there by interstate travellers. Inside there were two platforms, quiet and narrow, like a station in a small Javanese town. We took the "A" train, and then changed trains several times, and the subway stations gradually got bigger and noisier the closer we got to the center. We emerged through long alleyways of steps and New York was there in front of us: an exuberant city.

We went straight to the HRW office at 42nd Street and Fifth Avenue. HRW shares the third floor with a couple of other organizations with similar concerns: human rights, democracy, freedom of the press – all just ordinary problems in third-world countries. Despite HRW's sincere concern about these problems, its office seems so remote – an entire world away. I can't imagine how the people who work there – having never experienced such problems themselves – can have a feel for what is happening so far away – the violence, and the humor too, that happens there. Could they really believe it possible that a young woman like Marsinah might be brutally beaten and left to die for having the audacity to question the fairness of her wages? Can they imagine how they would feel about the intelligence investigation that followed her murder and that resulted in innocent people being tortured until they falsely confessed – thereby enabling the real murderer to get off scot-free?

At the same time, people in the office also seem to have an exaggerated notion of the effectiveness of an oppressive system like the one in Indonesia; they don't seem to realize, for example, that it's not all that difficult to obtain the books of Pramoedya Ananta Toer and other banned authors. Or that you can throw a small party for your friends in jail and give them a laptop computer or a mobile phone!

I don't see Indonesia as you do, as a machine of oppression. Instead, I envisage our country as swirling with unpredictability, a place where the law oscillates like a pendulum. At one end, there seems to be complete inefficiency, or maybe a sort of unwillingness to act. Whatever name you give it, people like to call it "negotiation". In the middle, there is law enforcement. And at the other end are all the excesses. In such a system, there's no such thing as receiving equal treatment regardless of who you are. Nor similar treatment regardless of the circumstances. The authorities have the power to buy or manipulate anyone. Sometimes people like you and I can bargain with them, at other times we're just the playthings of over-acting government agencies. And then there are those who are perpetually victimized – and they are always the poor. Why is that? When I think about the predicament of the poor, I can't help but wonder if God is just or if He exists at all.

It feels strange to be so remote from the problems that have been such a part of my life for so long. And I don't feel at home in my new habitat. They say that lots of people fall in love with this city the minute they arrive; but whether it's because I've only been here for a week or because I'm not a city boy at heart, I'm ambivalent. I feel like an extraterrestrial species here. And my work is going to involve mountains of paperwork and reports of human-rights violations thousands of kilometers away. I'm going to miss my friends in Sumatra, and the plantation and factory as well – not to mention you! I sometimes wonder whether I made the right decision. Might it have been better to have found a safe house in Indonesia? I did the previous time the authorities were after me. It's not that I'm not grateful to you and everyone else who helped get me here safely; I'm simply afraid that I won't be very useful here, especially when compared to what all of you are doing at home. Maybe there's more I could be doing in Indonesia.

And how are things there, especially in Medan? I've just started reading the files on the demonstration in Medan two weeks ago, the incident that was the catalyst for my fleeing here. From what I can make out, it seems a lot of people didn't quite understand what was happening and became uncertain about which side to take. Getting six thousand workers to demonstrate was an incredible feat by Indonesian standards, especially where the military has *ochlosophobia*, a fear of crowds. But all the public sympathy was instantly destroyed when racism reared its ugly head. The death of that Chinese businessman greatly distressed me.

The crowd's anger might have been sparked by years of injustice, but I still find it frightening to see how easily such anger can turn into racial hatred. I think we should have learned from prior experience about the flaws of mass action. Thousands of individuals in a crowd can suddenly become a herd with its own mentality. It takes only a single *agent provocateur* (not necessarily even an intelligence agent) to start stirring things up, and the crowd will follow his lead, like a herd of goats obeying a sheepdog. Then they can no longer distinguish the sheepdog from the wolf. Haven't we repeatedly said that that's what happened in the Malari incident? If someone sends out the cry to burn Chinese shops or destroy Japanese cars, suddenly hundreds of people are doing just that.

Of course we're in a difficult situation because we don't condone violence. There is absolutely no justification for it, and violence simply backfires. Whatever the justification and however much we are provoked, violence would only result in our actions being branded as terrorism and us being labelled criminal or subversive. Violence by the police and the army is deemed legal in the name of security and development. That is what they call the law. Perhaps it's time for us to abandon mass action in favor of other strategies including sabotage if there is no loss of life.

But getting back to the Medan case: does it look as if the State prosecutors will invoke the subversion clause? It's been two weeks. I hear that Mayasak was arrested and tortured. Have they allowed him legal representation? Do you have access to him? Give my regards to him if you do, and to Mochtar. I was most impressed by him when we met in Medan in March, when he was giving his lectures to the workers. He would be on the wanted list for sure, wouldn't he? Am I still on it? From time to time it occurs to me that running away was a pretty gutless thing to do. Please pass on my apologies for my not being there with you all. Sometimes I feel it wouldn't matter if I were caught. Why should I run away? Am I not a coward?

All this plays on my mind a great deal. At least I have one goal: to find some funds while I'm here to set up a network among the more remote areas. As we know, repression and torture in the provinces is always far worse than it is in Jakarta. Do you remember what happened to the people from Palembang Legal Aid at Muara Enim court that time? Someone punctured the tires on their car when they demanded a pretrial for the police chief of Perabumulih.

In Jakarta you hardly ever hear about journalists being abducted and tortured. But it happens in the provinces.

Yasmin,

I'm writing this letter in Sidney's apartment. I'm still sponging off her, but I'll be moving next week – to a lower-rent place in Brooklyn (an area I only know from the map). I've got a laptop now, with a modem and Internet connection. Or maybe it's a notebook; I don't know what the difference is. My friends in Singapore gave it to me, so I could fax them. But I've been using it to write my diary. Something quite new for me. I've never kept a diary in my life, apart from some notes about things that were going on at the plantation that I thought might be useful one day. I've always thought keeping a personal diary was too romantic and a sentimental sort of notion. Maybe that's the way I'm feeling these days. I'm lonely, I know that. Would you mind phoning my father and telling him I'm OK? He bought a new computer a while ago, a Pentium I think, to replace his old one. It would be terrific if he and I could keep in touch by email. He must be lonely too.

Thanks, Yasmin. And please pass on my best wishes and thanks to Cok for taking such a huge risk in smuggling me out of Medan. You two have a wonderful friendship.

Fondly,

Saman

PS: How are things with your husband?

From: Yasmin Moningka <yasmin_moningka@hotmail.com>
To: Saman <wisang@ibm.net>
Date: Sun, 8 May 1994 11:15:09 +0700
Subject: Re: New York

Saman,

Thank God! I'm so relieved to know that you're safe. You have no idea how worried I've been these last couple of weeks. I'd had no news of you since we said our farewells in Pekanbaru. It was as if you'd vanished into thin air. I couldn't even make contact with the friends who were going to meet you. I was worried that you had been arrested or that your boat had sunk. I prayed the rosary constantly. Lukas finally asked me why, and I told him that this is May and I was praying for all my friends who'd been arrested. I'm so glad to know that you are now safe in New York.

You shouldn't be too hard on yourself for fleeing. Yesterday I was reading a *Tempo* interview with Amosi from wherever he's hiding. He too chose to escape. He said that he did it because if he'd stayed he would be arrested and tortured without charges, like what always happened every time there was a demonstration. Nearly all the legal aid offices around Medan are empty now. Everyone's lying low. And, as we suspected, the ones who were arrested have been tortured. The charge is still subversion. In circumstances such as these, your wisest move is to get away. Anyway you can do a lot more from America than you can from jail, can't you? So I'll say it again – don't be hard on yourself.

I've been in Medan for the last three days. Things are getting back to normal although there's still a significant military presence. The factories are starting to operate again and the shops have re-opened. I'm going back to Jakarta tomorrow. I have to do a legal audit on a company that wants to go public. Dad has been great. He's letting me give some of my time to the legal aid team, on condition that I get my office work done too – he's reduced my load (and my bonus too, worse luck! But it doesn't matter, I don't want to get the other lawyers upset). In dad's view I still need money and a career. Without money we can't help ourselves or others. And I still have to do my job properly so dad won't be ashamed of me.

Otherwise it might be construed as nepotism.

If you really are keeping a diary, Saman, how about sharing it with me? Lukas won't see it. Even though we're husband and wife, we're careful about encroaching on each other's privacy. I miss you. I really do. I've run into a few friends from Perabumulih. They miss you too. I understand them when they say they love you. We all love you. And yes, I'll get in touch with your father as soon as I return to Jakarta tomorrow. I'll tell him he really should get an email address. You've never said anything to him about me, have you?

Fondly,

Yasmin

PS: Do you still think about me?

From: Saman <wisang@ibm.net>
To: Yasmin <yasmin_moningka@hotmail.com>
Date: Tue, 10 May 1994 23:05:50 -0500
Subject: My Diary

Yasmin,

How could I forget you?

Of course you can read my diary – the edited version, that is. I'm not going to send you the whole works. Not because it contains things you don't need to know – is there anything I can withhold from you? – but because of references to people whose names mustn't be revealed; even the Internet isn't secure. I'm going to install some additional security software. They call it "Pretty Good Privacy". But until I do you should always use an overseas provider. I know it's more expensive using the international rate (but as if it would matter to you!) You can never be sure that providers in Indonesia aren't being bugged by the government. And legally. too! Just ask Consumer Affairs. If necessary find out who has shares in the provider companies.

Anyway, here's my diary:

16 April – Medan. The situation is tense. The streets are deserted, even in daylight. Everyone is too scared to leave their houses, no businesses are open. The workers' demonstration has been going on for two days now and it seems that it's starting to fall apart. Innocent shop owners have had their premises trashed, and the worst came when an ethnic-Chinese businessman, Yuly Kristanto, was attacked and murdered by the crowd. Anti-Chinese pamphlets have been circulating ever since the first day. I don't know where they're coming from – probably intel. Early this evening we met secretly to evaluate the situation. We all felt defeated. The crowds are out of control. There's been a plethora of gossip and speculation, and we've concluded that the military is about to crack down. And with good cause. I have learned I'm regarded as one of the ringleaders, and my name is on a blacklist that has already been sent to the immigration office. We dispersed before nightfall, before the fugitives came under even more suspicion.

17 April – The military has been patrolling the streets since dawn, making it impossible to leave the city. Their shadows were visible as the sun rose. Raids are taking place throughout Medan, and spies are everywhere. I'm hiding out at a friend's shop. The others have split up and gone off to separate hiding places.

18 April – The military patrols have restored a modicum of security, and some roadside businesses have begun to reopen. Yasmin suddenly turned up, straight from Rosano's hearing in Palembang, dressed like a Chinese hooker from Singapore. She was wearing skin-tight leopard-spot pants, a black plastic jacket, and huge sunglasses. I didn't even recognize her. Turns out she had disguised herself as a business colleague of the friend whose boutique I'm staying in.

Yasmin's father learned from police headquarters in Jakarta that my name is on the five-most-wanted list. Yasmin urged me to flee the country. She said it wasn't just her own opinion, but that everyone else is saying the same thing. As it happens, Human Rights Watch is looking for someone to set up an information network in Southeast Asia, and she virtually forced me to accept the position. Everyone else agrees I should do it, she said. I feel under a great deal of pressure – there's no time to think about it. I know that the longer I stay here, the harder it will be to leave. (While there are may be plenty of evil people in the world, I'm surrounded by good people who always watch out for me.)

19 April – Yasmin came back to my hideout this morning in the company of a stylishly-dressed Malay woman. Like Yasmin and Laila, she was a former pupil of mine at Tarakanita High School. Three school kids – now all grown-up! It suddenly dawned on me that I'm nearly thirty-seven. I can't really picture them as kids, except for Laila – I got to know her through the letters she often sent me. And now Yasmin is organizing everything for my departure from Indonesia. Yasmin decided that this woman, Cok, should be the one to accompany me out of Medan. I was dubious at first because I hardly know her. But Yasmin obviously had utmost faith in her friend. The two of them took very seriously their job of disguising me. First they attached a false moustache, then shaved my hair and plucked my eyebrows to give them a new shape. They made me look as much as possible like the photo on an ID belonging to one of the workers at Cok's hotel in Pekanbaru. Yasmin had organized everything in her usual efficient manner.

My heart was in my throat as we backed the car, a Honda Accord, out of the garage. I sat in the rear, playing the role of an unassuming houseboy. None of the policemen we passed took any notice of me. Their eyes were only for the two sexy women in the front seat.

Tonight we're staying at the luxurious lake Toba International Hotel. Tomorrow we'll leave in a different car. To make it harder to keep track of us, they said. (Successful deception is costly. I don't know what a person without money or rich friends would do.)

20 April – Leaving Medan. We were stopped just as the car went onto Kapitan Patimura Street. We didn't know if the men who stopped us suspected something or just wanted to leer at the gorgeous women. Yasmin and I were nervous as kittens. I was worried that my disguise would be uncovered and the two women would be dragged into my crime. But Cok was all confidence and charm as she peppered her conversation with the names of high-ranking officials and business colleagues. They let us through without asking to see Yasmin's or my ID. We avoided the road to Pematangsiantar and stayed the night at Tarutung. I can't help out with the driving because I don't have a licence. The two women are unfazed by the atmosphere of high tension, which instead seems to have made our flight an adventure for them.

21 April – We got to Pekanbaru this afternoon and are now staying at Cok's hotel – the Pedussi Inn – in a bungalow suite with two bedrooms and a living room; we'll plan the rest of the journey here. For now, Cok has gone off to attend to some business arrangement so it's just Yasmin and me here tonight. We've already made some contacts. My plane leaves from Pekanbaru on the morning of the 24th. I'll meet the boat that same day.

22 April – Cok's not back yet. We've only had one phone call from her. What can be keeping her? For a second night, the two of us sat around talking. The day after tomorrow I will have to depart (wish me luck). If everything goes according to plan, I'll stay in the U.S. for a year or two. If not, I'll be here, languishing in jail

anywhere from three to thirteen years, depending on what legal clause the authorities invoke – subversive or criminal. When this possibility dawned on her, Yasmin started to cry. I held her in my arms to comfort her. She wept inconsolably, like a child, and I held her tighter. Then, rather incomprehensibly, I became the child and buried myself between her exposed breasts, like a hungry baby. We pressed close together. I was trembling. It was over before it started. I had no time to fathom what was happening. But Yasmin seemed to have no qualms – she led me to the bedroom. I don't know how I did it. When it was over, I felt so ashamed. But I was also overcome by relief and fell into a deep sleep.

In the middle of the night I was woken up because something was biting me near my armpit. I saw her fingers masturbating. She climbed on top of me after she finished. I knew that I don't know how to satisfy her.

23 April – I woke up feeling bewildered. Since leaving the parish, I hadn't given much thought to relinquishing my vows. And now here I am, covered in love-bites. I really don't understand how Yasmin could be attracted to a scrawny, unkempt body like mine. She's so beautiful. All day long she marked my body with bites. I'm like a caged mongoose, covered in dark spots. She's sapped me of all my strength.

24 April – Cok finally showed up, apologetic, to take us to the airport. She deliberately avoided looking at my neck. I was so embarrassed; I kept my head bowed the whole time. I didn't want to leave, and Yasmin cried again. But the plane had arrived.

25 April – I can still feel her body. I crave your body, Yasmin.

28 April – Made it to Singapore with no problem. There I was

given a laptop, and I started to write – mainly for the pleasure of reminiscing about what had just happened to me. A friend organized my ticket and visa. I've been so well looked after.

3 May – Landed at JFK Airport, where I was met by Ferouz Hasan, a Bangladeshi who had come to the States on a scholarship from Harvard Law School and now works freelance for Amnesty International and HRW. He's very smart; and it's a great comfort to have him around. He too hails from a country where human rights are a luxury. (Of course an Indonesian millionaire is far richer than the richest Bangladeshi! I have no doubt that the richest person in Indonesia is among the top ten richest people in the world.) On the subway, he talked at length about the fact that in his country people have to confront not only the military and the bureaucracy, but also terrorist political thugs. Neither of us has given up hope, however. Hope is our abiding comfort. "It is better to light a candle than to curse the darkness." My friends at HRW were pleased to see me. I felt the tension lift off my shoulders. I felt, though, that I had lost Indonesia and my friends there who had no choice but to stay and deal with an insidious system. (I've always been blessed by loving supportive friends, and by greater opportunities than others have. How can I use this abundance of good fortune to pay them back?)

8 May – I've just been to a seminar on Indonesia at Columbia University. It helped the homesickness a bit. There were quite a few people there. Sri Bintang came, he's here to see his son as well. And Buyung. Among the Americans there was a federal court judge and a Democratic member of Congress. A doctoral student by the name of Diyanti Munawar gave a paper on economic issues. I was interested in her perspective. When an American participant asked whether U.S. consumers should be boycotting Indonesian-made products such as Nike shoes, which are produced using exploitative industrial

practices, she replied that it would only hurt the workers. As soon as a boycott was in place, the foreign company would move its capital to some other country, like China, where there is an abundance of cheap labor. She pointed out that Indonesia's major problem is excess manpower: in its labor-intensive economy, most people can find work, but for low wages. On the other hand, increasing wages means reducing the number of people who can be employed, hence an increase in unemployment. The competition from other Asian countries makes things even more difficult. From the workers' point of view, however, a meagre wage is still better than unemployment. But then someone in the audience – I think he may have been from the Jakarta branch of the Indonesian Labor Welfare Union – said that while most companies in Indonesia claim that they can't afford to pay workers an appropriate wage, a significant percentage of their budget consists of "hidden costs", such as bribes to officials and functionaries.

I met Romo Martin, a Jesuit priest who is doing his PhD at Columbia, writing his thesis on the influence of Nuruddin Araniri on religious thought in Aceh. He was in fact one of the organizers of this seminar.

9 May – Day two of the seminar. A young presenter, Trulin Nababan, gave a paper on gender issues. She drew an interesting analogy between the attitude of the New Order to women and the organizational structure of the Indonesian Armed Forces. Giving women social and women's affairs portfolios is on par with the strategies of Dharma Wanita, the organization for the wives of military personnel. It is merely an extension of a patriarchal household where women are cocooned in domestic affairs, always assuming a nurturing role and leaving strategic decision-making entirely in the hands of men. Trulin believes that the very creation of a women's affairs portfolio is a denial of the fact that women's

issues are a joint political responsibility. She decried the attitude of the New Order government, which perceives women's issues as concerning women alone and not requiring men to take any responsibility. Trulin gave the example of marital rape, which has always been regarded as a private domestic matter. The reluctance to acknowledge that marital rape is an issue everyone must be concerned about, she said, is tantamount to refusing to acknowledge that women's rights are a subset of human rights. But an older woman in the audience objected, arguing that the very notion of marital rape is nonsensical because it is a wife's duty to serve her husband sexually. She said the hierarchical structure of a family often denounced by feminists keeps a man and woman's love for each other strong. The notion of "woman-as-object" is misguided, she said, because within such a structure the woman is "an object of love". Trulin responded by maintaining that all of Indonesia's problems originate in a patriarchal power structure. The two women could not reconcile their differences and the moderator had to step in to change the topic.

During the coffee break, I chatted with a federal judge by the name of Benjamin Silberman, a Jew who immigrated to America after his father died at Buchenwald. He is convinced that sexual Puritanism is making a big comeback in the USA. He sees a strange paradox in a feminism that declares "the personal is political" and "the domestic is socially constructed." The result, he said, is that the "personal" ceases to exist, having been subsumed by ideology. He told me about a single parent who had her children taken away from her because a social worker saw her six-year-old son patting her ten-year-old daughter on the backside. To the social worker, this was sexual harassment, and the mother was brought to court for failing to raise her children properly. There was also the case of the teenage couple who committed suicide. When the boy was seventeen and the girl almost fifteen they began a sexual relationship and decided to get married. Their parents approved but because the girl was below the age of consent and the boy was an adult, he was sent to jail. No consideration was given to the feelings or decision of the couple themselves. It's as if humans no longer have the right to regard their own behavior as something unique and individual. (Sex is clearly never a straightforward matter. I was reminded of Upi. I was reminded of myself.) As I was leaving Martin invited me to dinner tomorrow, at the Jesuit house.

10 May – I happily took up Martin on his invitation to dinner. The Jesuit House occupies two floors of an apartment building on the Upper West Side. It's an old building, a bit faded, with huge wooden doors. I was reminded of the parish house at Bogor Cathedral, where I lived for a while. Most of these Jesuits are Irish, but two are from the Philippines. I shared their regular evening meal and then we sat around, drinking Guinness and talking. A number of the Jesuits here have been frequent targets of police interrogation because of their involvement in demonstrations: anti-nuclear, anti-violence, anti-abortion. But of course the Church here doesn't have the political problems it faces in Indonesia.

I felt protected in their company; I felt I could share my hopes as well as my despair. Martin understands my disillusionment with the Church, but pointed out that large organizations inevitably become static and repressive. Therefore, there is little to be gained by leaving such an organization and trying to build a new one; after the new one has become established, it too will become static and repressive. All our energy will go on doing the very things we were initially protesting about. A self-liberating organization is a contradiction in terms. Our best hope is to humbly (or perhaps warily?) accept things as they are, but at the same time continue on our own journey. Perhaps this is the reason Jesus was always wary of organizations?

Sometimes I long to be like them once more: believing and hoping in a common cause, and supporting each other in making choices which, though difficult sometimes, are at the same time empowering, generating great passion. After all, to live a life of self-restraint has a pulse all its own. The yearning has been particularly poignant of late.

From: Yasmin Moningka <yasmin_moningka@hotmail.com>
To: Saman <wisang@ibm.net>
Date: Fri, 13 May 1994 20:39:41 +0700
Subject: Re: My Diary

Saman,

Please forgive me. Because you left the diocese, changed your name, changed your appearance, and so often expressed doubt even in God's existence, it never occurred to me that you might still harbor a desire to return to the priesthood. I don't know how to go about asking you to forgive me; for the last two days I've been putting off replying to your letter. I'm really sorry. Do you think of me as Eve seducing Adam?

From: Saman <wisang@ibm.net>
To: Yasmin <yasmin_moningka@hotmail.com>
Date: Sat, 14 May 1994 07:17:32 -0500
Subject: Re: Re: My Diary

Yasmin,

Don't you know that for centuries that story inspired decrees of injustice upon women? People live in tremendous fear of sexuality, but men do not want to be blamed for their desire, so we transfer the sin to women. But yes, you seduced me.

From: Yasmin Moningka <yasmin_moningka@hotmail.com>
To: Saman <wisang@ibm.net>
Date: Sun, 15 May 1994 01:47:12 +0700
Subject: Re: Re: Re: My Diary

Saman,

Was that a sin?

From: Saman <wisang@ibm.net>
To: Yasmin <yasmin_moningka@hotmail.com>
Date: Mon, 16 May 1994 06:39:22 -0500
Subject: Re: Re: Re: Re: My Diary

Yasmin,

I no longer know if there is such a thing as sin. Sex is too wonderful. Perhaps it made God so jealous that he ordered Moses to stone the adulterers?

But women have always been punished more vehemently. What about the woman stoned to death by the Pharisees outside the walls of Jerusalem – where did the men she slept with disappear to? I love you. I love you. I don't want you to get into trouble. You are so beautiful; you make me think of The Song of Solomon:

Thy stature is like to a palm tree, and thy breasts to clusters of grapes.

I said, I will go up to the palm tree, I will take hold of the boughs thereof.

From: Yasmin Moningka <yasmin_moningka@hotmail.com>
To: Saman <wisang@ibm.net>
Date: Fri, 20 May 1994 20:15:18 +0700
Subject: The Birth of Obed

For Saman:

From a foreign land two women returned to Bethlehem. Two widows, a mother and her daughter-in-law. And the name of the old woman was Naomi. White was her hair. Her husband had died in Moab. The young one, dark was her hair, was Ruth. Her husband had also died in Moab. The barren sands of the faraway country had swallowed their men, and they were left with no progeny. Naomi went on to return to the land of Judah, but Ruth clave unto her.

"Call me Mara because the Almighty has made my life very bitter," the old woman said to the townsfolk. "I went away full but I have come back empty." She had forgotten that Ruth was always by her side.

It was the beginning of harvest season. Thus Ruth went in search of a kindhearted landowner who might let her glean from his field ears of corn to feed herself and her mother-in-law for they had become very poor and they owned no more land. She entered the field belonging to Boaz, and the man took pity on her. He let the young woman gather after the reapers, and his men were not allowed to touch her. He told them to let fall some of the handfuls so she might glean the grains until nightfall. Then Ruth returned to her mother-in-law with an ephah of barley.

Naomi raised her face toward the sky. "Blessed be the man who has looked after us."

But the old woman told her daughter-in-law to bathe and dress herself up, because that evening Boaz, the blessed one, would be winnowing barley on the threshing floor. "Come, my daughter-in-law, wash and perfume yourself and put on your best clothes. Then go to the threshing floor, but don't let the man know you are there until he has finished taking his food and drink. When he lies down, note the place where he is lying. Then go to his side, uncover his feet, and lie down."

Ruth did as her mother-in-law told her. She doused herself with scented oil and lay in wait for Boaz behind a pile of wine jugs and gourds until he was asleep at the end of the pile of corn. She came quietly and watched his serene closed eyes. Then she turned back the cloak that was covering his feet and lay her head down. Her hair was untied. But she did not close her eyes.

In the middle of the night, something startled the man and he turned and discovered a woman lying at his feet. "Who are you?" he asked.

"I am your servant, Ruth," she replied. "Please spread the corner of your garment over me, Master, and protect me."

(And Boaz spread out his robe and covered Ruth. And she lifted her sheet so that he could get under it. They kissed a thousand times and lay in each other's arms on the straw.)

And then Boaz said to her, "The Lord bless you, my daughter, because you have not run after young men, neither the rich nor the poor, but rather have shown your love for me. Lie here until morning."

Thus Ruth came to know Boaz, and he rescued her from her troubles and her barrenness. He married her, and she gave birth to a son, a kinsman-redeemer for Naomi.

And the women of Bethlehem clamored to Naomi, "Praise be to the Lord for giving you a daughter-in-law who loves you though your hair has turned white. Such a woman is worth more than seven sons." They named the new baby Obed. Later Obed bore a son named Jesse and Jesse bore a son named David.

From: Saman <wisang@ibm.net>
To: Yasmin <yasmin_moningka@hotmail.com>
Date: Sat, 21 May 1994 09:15:59 -0500
Subject: Re: The Birth of Obed

Yasmin,

In his old age, Judah also had a daughter-in-law, but his firstborn son, Er, was wicked in God's sight and God slew him, thereby leaving the man's wife, Tamar, a widow. In line with tradition, Judah married his second son to Tamar in order that she might produce offspring for this son. But because Onan knew that Tamar's offspring would not be recognized as his own, whenever he lay with her he spilled his seed on the ground. What he did was wicked in God's sight and so he, too, was put to death. Thus Tamar was widowed for the second time. (This is the etymology of the words "error" and "onanism".)

As it happened, Judah had another son, a young boy called Shelah. But he was loath to give this boy to Tamar because he suspected that Tamar was a harbinger of death and he did not want Shelah to suffer his brothers' fate. He told Tamar to return to her father's house and promised her that he would give Shelah to her as soon as he became a man. But though she waited for quite some time, Shelah did not come to her. Tamar realized that her father-in-law did not intend to keep his promise to her and consequently she would have no offspring.

When she heard that Judah was going to Timnath to shear his sheep, she took off her widow's clothes, covered herself with a veil, and then sat down at the entrance to Enaim, which is on the road to Timnath, where her father-in-law would pass.

When Judah passed by, he assumed Tamar was a prostitute, for she had covered her face. He looked at her and said, "Let me come in unto thee."

Tamar asked, "What will thou give me, that thou mayest come in unto me?"

To which he replied, "I will send thee a sheep."

"Then thou must give me something as a pledge until thou send it: your seal, your bracelets, and the staff in your hand."

These things he gave to her and so she slept with him and became pregnant by him.

When in Timnath, Judah sent his friends with a young sheep back to Enaim. But they failed to find the prostitute who was at the entrance to Enaim. Further, news was heard that his daughter-in-law was with child through prostitution.

"Bring her to me," Judah ordered, "and have her burned to death!" His men then left to drag the woman to the fire.

But Tamar showed the seal and bracelets and staff of the man who had impregnated her. And Judah realized that he had gone back on his promise to his daughter-in-law. "She is more righteous than I, for I gave her not to Shelah my son," he confessed. But he did not sleep with her again.

When the time came for her to give birth, there were twin boys in her womb. As she was giving birth, one of them put out his hand, so the midwife took a scarlet thread and tied it on his wrist and said, "This one came out first." But he drew back his hand and his brother was born first. And he was named Perez. And the brother who had the scarlet thread on his wrist was given the name Zerah.

From: Yasmin Moningka <yasmin_moningka@hotmail.com>
To: Saman <wisang@ibm.net>
Date: Mon, 23 May 1994 07:49:43 +0700
Subject: Re: The Birth of Obed

Saman,

Why were progeny so important to the Israelites? I'm not pregnant yet. Do you think I could try making a test-tube baby?

From: Saman <wisang@ibm.net>
To: Yasmin <yasmin_moningka@hotmail.com>
Date: Sat, 28 May 1994 09:01:39 -0500
Subject: Two answers

Yasmin,

I have two answers – one lewd and one not. The lewd one: can I help to impregnate you?

The unlewd one: the Catholic Church still opposes test-tube babies. Why don't you just adopt a street kid, who has irreversibly been born into this condemned world?

From: Yasmin Moningka <yasmin_moningka@hotmail.com>
To: Saman <wisang@ibm.net>
Date: Mon, 30 May 1994 07:49:43 +0700
Subject: Re: Two answers

Saman,

So now you see birth as a matter of irreversibility. You are no longer the one I met when still in school, one who believed that life was a blessing designed by God. How old were you then? Twenty-two, twenty-three? Now I'm older than you were then. You lived for so long in Sumatra, now I find you've returned a different man, one who regards this world as condemned. A man who frequently has doubts about God. But a man who still has love. Laila was crazy about you, now I'm the one who is missing you.

About your suggestions: the second sounds more practical and socially responsible. But to be honest, I'd prefer the first. I want a baby from your tube. Is that a sin or not?

From: Saman <wisang@ibm.net>
To: Yasmin <yasmin_moningka@hotmail.com>
Date: Sat, 4 June 1994 08:58:11 -0500
Subject: Rabbis vs Ulemas

Yasmin,

(I am greatly confused about God. It's a doubt I can't talk to my father about. I'm his only child.)

You're always talking about sin. Of course we're committing a sin – at least towards your husband. The one consolation is that this sin we're committing is beautiful. Imaginative sin. At least for you and me it is. Even if procreation were a painful sacrificial act, I'd still give you a child if you asked for one. But of course that's pure hypothesis because sex is not a sacrifice, let alone a painful one. Sex is most confusing.

I've been reading a lot of literature about sex, the opinions and rules governing it, written by men over the centuries. The rabbis and the Church fathers believed that women were dangerous, lustful creatures who should be excluded. Meanwhile, the ulemas perceived that women were passive and sexually diffident, so it's only natural that a man should have more than one wife. But with you I now know that women and sexuality are something not easy to understand. Maybe they cannot be comprehended. Sometimes I feel like a virgin being deflowered, and I am in awe at the beauty of it. I'm not trying to blame you for the pleasure I'm experiencing. Even though it makes me confused.

From: Yasmin Moningka <yasmin_moningka@hotmail.com>
To: Saman <wisang@ibm.net>
Date: Thu, 9 June 1994 20:22:54 +0700
Subject: The Garden of Eden

For Saman:

In the Garden of Eden a man found himself lost in amazement. The moon was suspended above him. (The moon and the sky, they would become the only ageless beauty, said a child who was later born into the condemned world.) The sun had not yet set.

But the man was bewildered because one of his ribs was missing. Thus the voice of God had whispered to him. (They might have all been missing; he had not yet learnt anatomy). Where has my rib gone? Where could it possibly fall? But he beheld there, a leopard's leap away, a shapely figure with a pair of breasts, standing beneath the Tree of Knowledge. That's surely no animal, since it looks more like me (the man had seen his reflection in the pond the day before). But the tree is forbidden; the voice of God had whispered to him.

He approached the woman – as he would call her – and looked more closely. She stood there, like a young green shoot growing from the cambium. Her feet were bound in chains to a root thick and sinewy. The woman writhed.

"Even the animals in this park were created free, yet you are bound," said the man.

The woman squirmed as she tried to reach the dangling foliage. The fruit from the tree was red and shiny, dripping endlessly sweet droplets that turned into fresh moss and pebbles of onyx as it dropped onto the soil. The woman licked the fruit. She tried to bite into it but her hands were bound.

The man became angry and grabbed her flowing hair. "That is forbidden fruit!" (He didn't yet know that the woman was part of the tree.) The woman writhed and replied, "I'm just thirsty."

"I'm not allowed to even touch it. It's forbidden to me, so it's forbidden to you." The pious man raised his hand and struck the woman to the ground. "You must kneel and beg for forgiveness." (To whom, my lord?)

She bowed compliantly until the tips of her breasts touched the man's toes. She brushed his feet with her hair. Then she looked up, a tear in her left eye and a drop of blood in her right. Slowly she raised herself, grasping the man's leg, and stopped as she reached the top of his leg, where she found a furry patch like shrubbery. "Have mercy," she moaned. "I was merely thirsty. This fruit isn't forbidden, is it?"

The man did not reply. (God sent him no answer in the wind). The woman then bathed his shoot with her tears and soaked it with her saliva. The man squirmed as the bud ripened, and its veins blossomed within the warmth dampness between her tongue and palate.

The man's cries pierced the clouds as his milky seed spurted out. The drops didn't turn into jewels or sapphires, but a serpent slithered into his mind and cackled, "Delicious is sin," before his body had stopped trembling.

The world was silent. And the man became uncertain (where was God's voice?). Once again he seized the hair of the woman, as her tongue was still probing for the last drops of dew. The woman cried, "I was just thirsty."

"You have violated me. Torment and agony shall be your destiny!"

"I was thirsty. My lord, you know nothing about violation. You now nothing about confinement. You don't know the taste of sorrow nor sweat."

"But I can make them your destiny."

A passing stingray lent him its tail with which to beat the sinner.

Now that the man had whipped the woman's chest and back he discovered between her legs an orifice, from which emanated an enticing aroma. "You shall be called Woman because you were made from the rib of Man." Thus he was told by the whisper of God who suddenly reappeared. "And I will call these nipples because they are the tips of your breasts. And I will call this a clitoris because it is a petite phallus." But he didn't give the orifice a name. Instead he probed it with the tips of his fingers. And he penetrated it with his penis.

The woman squirmed but did not cry. Her breath was nearly finished. Her voice was finished. (I was just thirsty)

But the man was not finished with thrusting his penis, in full view of all the animals in the garden. (Later they would imitate it, and children would hear from their parents that it was a kind of war game). He thrusted his hips until his seeds sprayed into the orifice, from which emanated an enticing aroma. He groaned as a snake slithered from his brain, whispering: "Delicious is sin. But the woman has tasted the punishment."

But the clouds became calm, the howling beasts dispersed, when a Cherubim came to chase them away to the place where the sun sets. "I'm not just thirsty," said the man. "But also hungry."

From: Saman <wisang@ibm.net>
To: Yasmin <yasmin_moningka@hotmail.com>
Date: Sat, 11 June 1994 20:09:43 -0500
Subject: Re: The Garden of Eden

Yasmin,

I am masturbating.

From: Yasmin Moningka <yasmin_moningka@hotmail.com>
To: Saman <wisang@ibm.net>

Date: Sun, 12 June 1994 08:24:03 +0700
Subject: Re: Re: The Garden of Eden

Saman,

I have alloerotism. I have sex with my husband, but it's you I'm imagining. He's been asking why I so often want the lights out. It's because I'm imagining your face, your body.

From: Saman <wisang@ibm.net>
To: Yasmin <yasmin_moningka@hotmail.com>
Date: Mon, 13 June 1994 22:14:53 -0500
Subject: Comparisons

Yasmin,

I'm jealous. You're having sex, I'm not. Your husband is surely a better lover than I am? I come too fast. But I suppose if I were to get you pregnant, it would mean I am efficient – capable of getting a task done in a short time.

From: Yasmin Moningka <yasmin_moningka@hotmail.com>
To: Saman <wisang@ibm.net>
Date: Tue, 14 June 1994 07:42:44 +0700
Subject: Re: Comparisons

Saman,

Lukas has it down pat, yes. With him it feels like exercise. He changes position every time he's done four sets of eight strokes. How does that differ from an exhausting workout in the gym?

From: Saman <wisang@ibm.net>
To: Yasmin <yasmin_moningka@hotmail.com>
Date: Wed, 15 June 1994 23:10:51 -0500
Subject: Differences

Yasmin,

Climax. That's what makes it different. Be frank with me, you didn't have orgasm with me, did you?

From: Yasmin Moningka <yasmin_moningka@hotmail.com>
To: Saman <wisang@ibm.net>
Date: Thu, 16 June 1994 22:15:04 +0700
Subject: Re: Differences

Saman,

Orgasm through penile penetration is not the be-all and end-all. I always have an orgasm when I think about you. I come because of everything you are.

From: Saman <wisang@ibm.net>
To: Yasmin <yasmin_moningka@hotmail.com>
Date: Sun, 19 June 1994 08:19:11 -0500
Subject: Re: Re: Differences

Yasmin,

Maybe our sexual intercourse should remain in our imagination. Virtual sex. I don't even know how to satisfy you.

From: Yasmin Moningka <yasmin_moningka@hotmail.com>
To: Saman <wisang@ibm.net>
Date: Mon, 20 June 1994 22:15:04 +0700
Subject: Memory lessons

Saman,

You remember that night, that very night, when all I wanted was to caress your body and watch your face as you ejaculated? I want to come to you. I'll teach you. I'll rape you.

From: Saman <wisang@ibm.net>
To: Yasmin <yasmin_moningka@hotmail.com>
Date: Tuesday, 21 June 1994 07:55:49 -0500
Subject: Re: Memory lessons

Yasmin,

Teach me. Rape me.

also from
EQUINOX PUBLISHING

NON-FICTION

THE SECOND FRONT:
Inside Asia's Most Dangerous
Terrorist Network
Ken Conboy
979-3780-09-6
2005, softcover, 256 pages

WARS WITHIN:
The Story of *TEMPO*,
an Independent Magazine
in Soeharto's Indonesia
Janet Steele
979-3780-08-8
2005, softcover, 368 pages

SIDELINES:
Thought Pieces from
***TEMPO* Magazine**
Goenawan Mohamad
979-3780-07-X
2005, softcover, 260 pages

AN ENDLESS JOURNEY:
Reflections of an
Indonesian Journalist
Herawati Diah
979-3780-06-1
2005, softcover, 304 pages

SRIRO'S DESK REFERENCE
OF INDONESIAN LAW 2005
Andrew I. Sriro
979-3780-03-7
2005, softcover, 200 pages

BULE GILA:
Tales of a Dutch Barman
in Jakarta
Bartele Santema
979-3780-04-5
2005, softcover, 160 pages

THE INVISIBLE PALACE:
The True Story of a
Journalist's Murder in Java
José Manuel Tesoro
979-97964-7-4
2004, softcover, 328 pages

INTEL:
Inside Indonesia's
Intelligence Service
Ken Conboy
979-97964-4-X
2004, softcover, 264 pages

KOPASSUS:
Inside Indonesia's
Special Forces
Ken Conboy
979-95898-8-6
2003, softcover, 352 pages

TIMOR: A Nation Reborn
Bill Nicol
979-95898-6-X
2002, softcover, 352 pages

GUS DUR:
The Authorized Biography of
Abdurrahman Wahid
Greg Barton
979-95898-5-1
2002, softcover, 436 pages

NO REGRETS:
Reflections
of a Presidential Spokesma
Wimar Witoelar
979-95898-4-3
2002, softcover, 200 pages

FICTION

THE SPICE GARDEN
Michael Vatikiotis
979-97964-2-3
2004, softcover, 256 pages

THE KING, THE WITCH AND
THE PRIEST
Pramoedya Ananta Toer
979-95898-3-5
2001, softcover, 128 pages

IT'S NOT AN ALL NIGHT FAIR
Pramoedya Ananta Toer
979-95898-2-7
2001, softcover, 120 pages

TALES FROM DJAKAR
Pramoedya Ananta To
979-95898-1-9
2000, softcover, 288 pa

CPSIA information can be obtained at www.ICGtesting.com
Printed in the USA

267280BV00001B/2/A